Chivalry in the Monastery

Garner Fritts

Chivalry in the Monastery
by Garner Fritts

Printed in the United States of America

ISBN 9781606473887

www.xulonpress.com

Chapter One

"Get up Adrian!"

I opened my eyes and saw my red-haired uncle standing over me. I hadn't seen him for several months. Blood curdling screams of men, women, and children rang in my ears. I heard clay pots and utensils being smashed into the floor. The smell of burning hay and wood filled the room choking me. I leaped from my bed and put my mail shirt on. Uncle Ambrose's green eyes sparkled as he handed me an axe and looked toward the sound of the commotion. My uncle was fully dressed in his armor, except for his helmet.

"What is it lord?" I asked.

"The Mongols," he said. He twitched his mustache as if his nose were itching. "They're plundering all the nearby manors. The other knights were unprepared to engage them. They killed your master." He cut the air with his sword. "It will never be said that Ambrose died without a fight. It is the will of heaven that we stand against these pagans."

I clasped the axe tightly and swallowed hard. I couldn't imagine anyone defeating Sir Johns. I hardly knew him, serving Johns for only a month. I had heard of the Mongols. Some said these devils had an empire larger than any other on earth, and they were merciless.

"We must get to the horses or they'll slaughter us like pigs," Sir Ambrose said.

I followed him to the window. He lifted the linen draped over the bay with the edge of his sword.

I peered through the lattice. Three brutish men with thick mustaches and strange turbans rode through the estate with bows raised. Bells dangling from their waist jingled. They were shouting and laughing. Rumor was that they were ruled by a man known as the khan.

"All the horses are gone except for Galant," I said. I watched Sir Johns' prized stallion thrash violently, kicking dents into his stable door across from the yard.

Someone pounded on the door. I jerked with surprise, but Ambrose hurried over to the wall beside the entrance.

"Open it," he whispered.

I unlatched the door and stumbled backward from the force of the savage on the other side. Ambrose yelled a battle cry and struck the beast-like man in the shoulder.

The man bellowed in pain. I swung the axe and hit him in the chest. The weapon bounced off of him. He fell to the ground, writhing and rolling around across the floor. This pagan reeked of strong body odor. My hands were shaking, and I dropped the axe.

"Hurry!" Sir Ambrose said.

I hurdled the injured body and followed my uncle to Galant. The horse's fine coat gleamed in the sunlight beaming over the horizon. Galant bobbed his head up and down as we approached. My heart raced. I never turned back to look, but I heard coarse voices and ringing bells looming closer. I opened the gate and climbed on the stallion behind my uncle.

Ambrose clicked Galant's side with his heels, and the horse shot out of the stable like a stone launching from a catapult. I felt hands clawing at me from behind. I kicked them away, cringing at the thought of their rough, filthy hands touching me.

As we rode away from the estate, everything was in a blur. Fires blazed everywhere. All the barns, all the mills, all the houses, and every other dwelling billowed with thick black smoke. Flaming arrows whizzed by us. Peasants ran around wildly while being chased by the invaders. Bodies fell as their attackers preyed on them with their sabers. In an instant, all the hideous sounds faded in the distance behind us,

Sir Ambrose slowed Galant to a trot as we ventured into the forest. The early morning light gave way to a gray overcast sky. The only sounds were the croaking of nearby frogs, the steady trickling of a small stream, and the plopping of Galant's hooves along the green forest floor. A light breeze whistled through the trees and gently swayed the branches from side to side. Cool, misty raindrops kissed my face.

"I left everything," I said. I pressed my chin into my chest to keep the rain off my face. "We have no clothes except for what is on our backs, no food, no cloaks to protect us from the chilly rains, and no charms to ward off evil spirits in these woods."

"We don't need any," Ambrose said. "The Dayma Monastery is close by."

The bells of the Mongols rang behind us, disrupting the steady sounds of nature.

"They're looking for us," Sir Ambrose said. He clicked his heels against Galant's side, and the stallion trotted faster, splashing through the small puddles in his path.

"There's something I must tell you," Ambrose said with despair in his voice.

"What is it lord?"

"Your father. . .and mother. . . the Mongols. . .speared like animals. . ."

"When?" I asked. My voice quivered. I gritted my teeth to choke back tears, for a knight was not given to effeminate qualities like weeping. My father was the Baron of Granes. He was a chivalrous and pious man. Everyone liked him. He was dead, killed like a common slave by sinners?

"The bailiff from your father's manor brought me word," Sir Ambrose said. "He was the only one to survive. I suspect they allowed him to escape so he would unknowingly lead them to your master's estate." Ambrose shook his head. "I tried to warn Sir

Johns, but it was too late. There was no time to prepare a defense."

I clenched my fists until my nails dug into my palms. I wanted to turn around and take the Mongols on. I wanted to kill them all. I wanted to torture them like they had probably tortured my parents.

The ringing bells grew faint in the distance.

"Cowards! They fear the tree spirits!" I looked back through the dense trees. All I saw were a few leaves swirling in the wind. Misty rain gathered on small branches, making them bow slightly under the weight. Those drops splashed to the ground in larger droplets.

The chorus of the frogs grew louder than the enemy bells.

"Turn around or they will get away!" I said.

Ambrose didn't respond.

"I beg you!" I shouted louder. I growled and kicked like an angry child until I was breathing hard. Galant swayed and grunted, but Ambrose steadied him and remained silent.

"What would your father think?" Ambrose asked. He looked at me out of the corner of his eye. Water dripped off his big nose.

"I'm acting as a knight should," I said coldly. I wiped the raindrops off my face. "A true knight would strike down the enemies of God and not run away like a coward." I hoped to incite his sense of chivalry.

"A man of valor wouldn't attempt such a feat without the blessing of his king," Ambrose said.

"And the king doesn't act without the prompting of God."

I groaned. He was right. My father had told me of Ambrose's chivalry and of his great deeds done for the king and the church. But how could God allow my noble father to be murdered by insolent men like the Mongols? The instant an army was mustered, I wanted to be in the fighting.

Ahead of us was a clearing in the forest. Trees on either side bent in such a way as to form arches. A large building the color of sandstone stood erect behind a large gated wall in the clearing ahead. Near the top, a statue of the Holy Mother caressed the Child. There were several windows on what seemed to be upper and lower floors. Two massive doors stood beside one another. The gate was open, but the doors were bolted shut. It dwarfed any church I had ever seen. Ambrose halted Galant and dismounted.

"The Dayma Monastery," Ambrose said.

Chapter Two

I dismounted Galant and led him to where Ambrose stood. My uncle tapped the massive door with the bronze knocker. There was no answer.

"This is strange." Ambrose scratched his head. He knocked harder. In between knocks, the heavy doors creaked open. A pale man with a thin face, a bald scalp, and bulging eyes appeared.

"Do you bear any wounded?" the man asked.

Sir Ambrose shook his head.

"We have been busy lately," the monk said. "We've treated many wounded from the recent invasion of the Tartars." He motioned for us to enter. "Come to the abbot's quarters."

I followed Ambrose through the door while two other monks led Galant away. We walked down a pathway laced with beautiful flowers and trimmed bushes on each side. Light shimmered off the windows of the buildings, making squares of light on the ground. The buildings lined this outdoor garden on all four sides. The bulgy-eyed monk handed us dry cloaks to wear, then we entered the hallway of a building with an arched ceiling and pillars. The bulgy-eyed monk stopped and bowed low at the approach of another monk. The other monk was tall, heavy and bald. He limped on his left leg.

"Greetings in the name of our Lord," the large monk said. He turned to the bulgy-eyed monk. "Be sure to bring plenty of provisions for our guests."

The bulgy-eyed monk acknowledged the command, and with his head lowered toward the floor, disappeared in an instant.

"I am Peter," the large monk said. "I am the abbot of the Dayma monastery. How can we be of assistance to you?"

"I am Sir Ambrose," my uncle said. He placed his hand upon my shoulder. "This is Adrian, the son of Baron Andrew, my brother."

Peter smiled. "Ah yes! The great Baron of Granes. Few nobles are as godly as that man." Peter's deep voice bellowed as he spoke.

Sir Ambrose lowered his head. "I'm afraid my brother and his mistress were mauled by the invading Mongol tribes."

Peter signed the cross and muttered prayers for my family. I didn't know what he said or what my uncle told him thereafter. I turned toward the wall, hoping any moment to awaken from this nightmare. I wondered if anyone had properly buried my father and mother. The last thing I had said to my father was something unkind about keeping me from becoming a knight for so long. I was sixteen and merely a squire. I guess he had reason, but most men my age were entering knighthood. I felt guilty that I had spoken disrespectfully to my father. The only way I could make up for what I did was to avenge my parents' death.

"This is yours," the bulgy-eyed monk said, waking me out of my daydream. He placed a piece of warm bread and a cup of ale into my hands.

I hadn't eaten since yesterday, so it was a welcome sight. I bit into the bread and coughed with disgust. The bread tasted like cheap meal the peasants used in their ovens. Although I didn't want it, I nibbled on it so I wouldn't offend these monks. I ate and listened as my uncle and this abbot continued their conversation.

"Although they are Mongols, I don't think these vagrants are part of the Mongol empire," Ambrose said.

"You're right," Peter said. "Some of the wounded knights said they are renegades of the Golden Horde. They seek to make their own evil empire among us." Peter signed the cross again. "Mad devils! At least they respect our religious orders."

"They wear bells," Ambrose added. "I'll never forget that cursed ringing with every move they made."

I wouldn't forget it either. I flinched at the thought of that strong body odor they had.

"Will you be staying with us?" Peter asked.

"We've got to muster an army large enough to fight these invaders," Ambrose said. "They have taken Granes and ransacked several other counties.

Someone needs to reach the king before we lose the whole kingdom."

"Take whatever provisions you need for your journey," Peter said, "and may God be with you."

Ambrose kissed the hand of the abbot, and then turned to me. "Adrian?"

"Are we leaving now?" I was ready to go.

"You're not going with me," Ambrose said.

Not going with him? Did I not act bravely when we fought that Mongol? Wasn't I more courageous than he in my desire to attack the Mongols head on? It was my family they killed; I had to have revenge.

"Abbot, allow Adrian to stay with you until I return. He has the courage of his father but lacks the seasoning of an aged warrior."

"I'm going with you." I wasn't some helpless maid he could treat any way he wanted. Ambrose wasn't my master, and I didn't have to follow his orders.

"We only have one horse," Ambrose said. "If I were to engage in combat along the way, it would be difficult to fight with two riding." He straightened his glove. "Besides, you have no experience. I couldn't stand to see my nephew slain too."

What did he know of my skills? "I'm as good as any knight," I lied. I pointed toward the stables outside the monastery. "I can ride one of those horses."

"That breed is not a destrier like Galant. They wouldn't stand a chance in a fight. You have no weapon, no horse, and no experience. You cannot go."

"You will be safe with us," Peter said.

Ambrose walked toward the door. If I let him go, I was sure to never leave this place.

"You need me!" I shouted.

Ambrose stopped in front of the door but never turned around. "I'm sorry," he said. The bulgy-eyed monk opened the door for Ambrose, and he disappeared.

"He'll return," Peter said.

I felt trapped amid thick walls and raggedly dressed monks. Life as I had known it would be no more. This was now my home.

Chapter Three

"Adrian, if you are to remain among us, there are some rules you must follow."

I didn't look at Peter, but I nodded. I didn't see any point to this. One way or another, I planned on leaving soon.

He patted me on the back of the neck. "I know it is hard for you now my son, but wounds heal in time. The best thing you can do now is set your mind on things above, and not on these temporal things. We need to go over the most important rules right now. After that, I will assign another monk to you to teach you the rest." Peter took a bag filled with provisions and showed it to me. "No one can have private possessions. You will eat meals at the appointed times." He examined my rain-drenched clothing. "You must wear the adorning of the monks. Since the guest house has been demolished, you'll stay in the dormitory."

Obviously he didn't know what nobility was like. I never wore anything even closely resembling beggar's clothing. I always ate the finest foods and slept in the finest beds.

"You'll be given work to do each day, and there will be devotional reading and prayer."

I looked at this big, balding man towering over me as he continued his admonition. He seemed to be in deep thought, not once looking at my facial expressions. I had no intention of doing menial work or reading boring books. If I had to stay here for the moment, I needed time to practice my yard skills in preparation to fight the Mongols.

"Do you understand Adrian?"

I nodded again. I hoped he didn't ask me to repeat what he had said.

Peter smiled. "Good. Follow me to your dormitory and remain quiet along the way." He dragged his left leg as he walked.

I followed Peter down a pathway surrounded by a beautiful garden. We passed several buildings. I kept quiet, but I glanced into every open doorway. I saw a room where monks sat at desks and wrote with quills in hand. In another building, I saw wounded being cared for by more monks. I slowed my pace and squinted to see if I knew anyone in this infirmary. Perhaps there was someone in there that could help me. I wanted to work with the wounded so I could find out what is going on outside the monastery and perhaps find a way to leave.

We climbed stairs leading up to a number of rooms. Inside the first dormitory were two beds embedded into the wall opposite one another. The place was cool and damp. A table sitting in the middle of the room held a candle.

"Adrian, meet your new teacher."

The gray eyes of a scrawny, pale, dark-haired monk met mine. His scalp was shaved like the others. He smiled at me with a sheepish grin.

"This is Eli," Peter said. "He will teach you the monastic rules during your stay." Peter nodded to the both of us, and then he left.

I stared at this thin form watching me. Eli looked sickly. I must have looked at him strangely because his face grew flushed and he put his head down. One thing I didn't want was a cowardly keeper spying on my every move. Eli extended another robe out to me draped over his gangly arms. I glanced at it and then sat down on the floor. Eli laid the garment neatly on my bed and sat down opposite me with his arms crossed over his bent knees. He kept his head down and never said a word. I didn't care.

After a few minutes I stood up, stretched myself out, and climbed into bed. It was hard and cold, nothing like my soft straw bed next to Sir Johns' side. I turned toward the wall so I didn't have to look at Eli sitting there. I could've been sitting around a fire plotting with fellow soldiers on how to attack the Mongols. I was betraying my father.

I felt someone shake me, and I turned to see the greeting gaze of Eli.

"What is it?" I rubbed my eyes. "What time is it?"

"It is close to noon," Eli said softly. "You slept through Matins, Breakfast, Lauds, Prime, and Tierce. No one noticed. It is time for Chapter Mass and the Chapter Meeting. We will get our task for the day from the abbot."

This was my chance. "Eli, can we work in the infirmary?"

"That would be up to Abbot Peter," Eli said. "You must know how to use herbs to work there." His voice faded as he spoke.

I changed into my robe and followed Eli to the chapter. Monks filed into the building, and every one of them hung their heads down and kept silent. Peter went over the business of the monastery and then issued orders. Monks disappeared without delay as soon as they got their task. Eli and I stood before Peter. I bowed my head.

"Hmmm." Peter scratched his chin. "Let's put you both to sweeping the hallways."

Sweeping hallways? Couldn't I go to the infirmary? Eli had told me to never question the abbot. I never handled such utensils in my life, and I wasn't about to sweep any floors. We swept the storeroom next to the infirmary. I pushed the broom back and forth on the ground. Eli swept so hard there were dust clouds around him. I walked down the hallway toward the infirmary, slowly pushing my brush as I went. I saw Eli shaking his head at me. I looked away from him and pushed my broom forward.

As I entered the doorway to the infirmary, the infirmarian met me at the door shaking his head and pointing toward the hallway.

"The dust will add to their sickness," he said.

I saw two peasants and a few children lying on beds. There were monks crouched over them administering medicine and chanting prayers. When I knew I was out of sight, I carried my brush down the hallway to Eli. I handed him my broom, turned around, and headed to the dormitory.

I went to my quarters and sat there. I didn't care what Peter, Eli, my uncle, or anyone else thought. None of them understood. I stayed in my room for hours thinking about my family and what I had lost. Soon the evening shadows loomed large into the domicile.

Eli appeared in the doorway along with Peter. This was it. My scrawny teacher had tattled on me, and now I would be punished.

"Adrian," Peter said, "Eli tells me you've done quite well today. Very good." He walked out of the quarters.

I stared at Eli. Was there something wrong with him? Eli appeared to be more pious than the others. I stood to my feet. My body ached where I had sat for so long.

"Didn't he notice my absence?" I asked.

"I did your work," Eli said. "I covered for you during meals, recreation, and the services." He pulled some bread and a cup of ale out of his robe. "I brought you this."

I gorged the food and gulped down the drink like a starved dog. Some of the juice dribbled off my chin. "Why did you do this?" I asked.

Eli sighed. "I lost my parents to the Tartars too. They weren't killed, but they were enslaved. My sister escaped with me clutched in her arms. She brought me here as an infant. After being here for only one month, she died in the women's quarters of the Dayma monastery. I never saw my parents again."

I lowered my head in respect. "Who are the Tartars?"

"The Mongols," Eli said. "We call them Tartars. It is Latin from *Tartarus*. They are the children of hell."

"Thank you." I extended my hand to Eli. "I'm sorry I put you through that. I just want to get out of here."

"It's okay. I had a hard time at first." Eli squeezed my hand tightly. "God will help you with your grief as He helped me. Anytime you need to talk, I'll listen."

I saw Eli in a different light. He wasn't like the others. Eli was more devout, and he understood what I was going through. As I crawled into bed, I rested easier knowing I had someone who shared my pain.

Chapter Four

I rolled out of bed and followed Eli to the chapel. The monks were assembling on their knees chanting and praying. I knelt beside my new friend and found myself swaying toward him. Eli nudged me, and I shook myself to attention. My knees hurt from kneeling on the hard floor for so long. Eli helped me to my feet when the praying ended.

"Now we have breakfast," Eli said.

I followed my mentor to a building they called the refectory. Inside was a large table with benches on each side. A large chair sat at the head of the table, and a pulpit was close by with an open book lying on it. All the monks gathered around the table, blessed the food, and began to eat. Peter sat in the large chair, and another monk stood at the pulpit and read aloud in Latin. A server placed curds, bread, and ale before me. This wasn't worthy of my rank, and I had no idea what the monk behind the pulpit was reading. I had learned some French and Latin from the priest on my father's manor, but nothing like what I was hearing.

I pushed my plate to the side and tapped Eli. "Don't they have anything else to eat?"

The man at the pulpit no longer spoke. I looked around, and every monk at the table gazed at me. Eli's face flushed and he put his head down.

"Adrian, you know there is no talking during the meals," Peter said. "No one interrupts the reading of the Holy Word."

"It's my fault abbot," Eli said. "I didn't fully explain this to him."

That wasn't completely true. Eli had told me we were to remain silent during the meals, but he didn't tell me why. I started to protest, but Eli nudged me.

"Eli," Peter said, "you lose your eating privileges. Give me your food and stand up until breakfast is over."

Eli rose from his seat, walked over to Peter, handed his plate to the abbot, walked back, and stood over his seat with his head bowed. The speaker resumed his reading and everyone finished eating. I pushed my plate over in front of Eli. I wanted real food, and my friend didn't deserve to lose his meal. He stood there and wouldn't touch my offer. Peter watched me the rest of the time, but he didn't say anything.

After breakfast, I followed Eli along the cloister to a building larger than all the others. It was adjacent to the slightly taller bell tower. It rang with loud clanging for each service of the day.

"This is the nave of the chapel," Eli said. "We gather here for services."

The inside was impressive. Rows of benches covered each side of the nave. On the east side was a stone altar with three steps leading up to it. An altarpiece decorated the back of the pedestal. It was a picture of Christ and his disciples. Next to the holy piece stood elevated seats where monks gathered with books in hand. On the north side of the church, a large pulpit dominated the scene. We entered the aisle and stood near the front benches.

"This is High Mass," Eli whispered.

Although I didn't understand the Latin, the monks sang in unison and beautiful harmony. It reminded me of the songs of visiting minstrels. Their songs were different. They were about the great adventures of the knights. It reminded me of home. It reminded me that my father's blood was singing for me to honor his memory.

I saw the infirmarian sitting two rows back. If I could speak to him, maybe he could tell me about a recently wounded knight coming into the monastery, or maybe news about the preparation of the war against the Mongols. I shuffled my feet sideways while looking straight ahead. It made a grating noise along the floor. Eli watched me out of the corner of his eye, but he didn't move. I slid my feet along the ground, backing myself up until I was parallel with the infirmarian. He didn't look at me. I dragged my feet sideways until I stood next to him.

"Are there any knights among the wounded?" I whispered. I kept my eyes straight ahead. He never answered me, so I repeated the question louder. Again, he didn't answer. I elbowed him, and he ignored me.

I started toward my seat, keeping my eyes straight ahead when I bumped into something large to my left. I turned and saw Peter's angry glance.

"Follow me," he demanded, "and stay put until I give you audience."

While a monk took the stand to deliver homily, Peter pointed me to a small room with its own altar. A picture of a saint hung on the wall in front of the holy relic. I sat down in the corner and listened to the faint voice of the speaker.

After a while Peter limped into the room, and I stood up. He looked toward the picture, made the sign of the cross, and turned to me.

"If it were not for the threat of the Tartars, I'd send you to do the work of the lay brothers in the fields or make you stay in the guest quarters."

Peter had told me the guest quarters were destroyed. Had I not heard correctly? I kept my head down and said nothing.

Peter clasped his hands together. "I've been reserved toward you because you're a guest and you are ignorant of the holy methods. God and the church are the rule here. You obey fully and without question or you'll be punished."

"All I wanted to know is whether there are any wounded knights here," I said. "I intend to leave with them and find my uncle. I don't want to stay."

"This would be your privilege under normal circumstances," Peter said. "Christendom is at war, and anybody who isn't fighting must remain in a safe refuge. You can't leave until your uncle returns for you." Peter grabbed my arm and led me to the threshold. "Until then, follow the rules or face punishment."

I considered pulling out of his grasp, but I thought he might strike me. I'd heard that he had smitten other monks before; I wasn't so sure he wouldn't hit me. I went back to the dormitory and met Eli at the entrance.

"Why do you treat Abbot Peter like that?" he asked.

"I meant no irreverence," I said. "Religious rule has its place, but knightly rule doesn't bow to it."

"What do you mean?"

"Knights live under the code of chivalry. It's just as noble as the rule of the monastery. Depriving a knight of a fight is to deprive him of honor and all he stands for. Knights are the protectors of all Christendom." I slashed through the air as if I held a sword. "My father was a knight, my uncle is a knight, and I was to be a knight until the Tartars destroyed my master Johns' manor."

Eli sat down and leaned forward. "What was life like on the manor?"

"It depended on who you were," I said. "Peasants lived hard lives, but I was part of the nobles. I had servants to do the chores, bakers to cook the meals, maids to clean the cottage, and a priest who conducted Mass on the Lord's Day." I sighed. "Everyday my father let me dress him in his knightly attire. Let's see. . ." I pretended to put clothing on Eli's shoulders. "After asking him to stand by the fire, I held his shirt up to put his arms through."

Eli humored me and stretched his arms out.

"Then I put on the red tunic, and the hose, and the boots, and all the rest. My father looked magnificent. He took part in tournaments and won my mother's hand with an act of bravery. He won the respect of the king and got his own county."

I saw my father's face. Andrew had flowing blonde hair and a well-defined beard. He looked angelic. Many said I looked like him, except for the beard. I felt lonely. I had to change the subject.

"What was it like for you growing up in this place?"

"Well. . ." Eli ran his hand over his bald scalp. "The other monks have treated me with great care. Abbot Peter has been my greatest mentor. School days were ten hours long. I learned Latin, math, writing, prayers, hymns, music, science, and law. When I was thirteen, I had the chance to leave. I stayed and took the vows of poverty, chastity, and obedience. I've been here ever since."

"Why did you stay?"

"It was all I ever knew," he said. "Besides, I learned what was most important in life, and I found peace from my childhood troubles."

I admired Eli, and I believed what he said. I knew I would be a knight one day, but perhaps there was something I would learn from this place. I wanted the peace Eli had. As we went to the chapter meeting, I promised myself that I would find it.

Chapter Five

Over the next few weeks, things moved quickly. The warm spring days gave way to the blistering heat of the summer. I learned the Tartars were still advancing, and no one had been able to stop them. I wondered if my uncle had been killed. I tried to put it out of my mind and concentrated on learning the ways of the monk from Eli.

"Things are different here during the summer," Eli said. "There will be more study." He pointed to his head. "There will be two meals." He rubbed his belly. "There will be less sleep, but less work too." He pretended to sweep the floors. He was more talkative now than when I first met him.

"Why is Peter cruel to the monks?" I asked. "This morning he had someone chant prayers until his voice gave out."

"He isn't cruel," Eli said. "It's how we learn obedience. We must be humbled. Saying prayers is the most common penance given to us. There could be worse."

"Tell me."

"Once a man came to Nones late for three days in a row. He was whipped soundly." Eli rubbed his chin. "Another monk ate more portions than the others for weeks. When Abbot Peter found out, he made him and the server eat half of their normal portion on their knees and then push their plates back to the kitchen with their noses."

"Knights don't do such things to anyone. Not even their enemies." I raised my arm as if giving a battle signal. "My father was one of the most respected knights in any kingdom. The Tartars refused to show him that respect." I lowered my arm. "Do you see why I must leave and defend my father's honor?"

Eli shook his head. "Perhaps there was a higher purpose in what took place. There are mysteries which we are not meant to know." He peered at the sun through the window. "It's time for study. Abbot Peter asked me to teach you Latin and instruction from the Holy Scriptures. We'll go to the scriptorium, and you must be quiet."

As we walked into the cloister, the heat from the noon-day sun beamed onto my face. Beads of sweat surfaced on my forehead and trickled down my cheeks. Other monks entered their respective places with their heads down. I wondered if anyone ever bumped into anything like that. Eli chanted a prayer in Latin as we went. I made the sign of the cross. I felt a peace inside whenever I heard Eli pray. I wanted to learn one of those prayers.

It was my first visit to the scriptorium. Monks sat in chairs lined up across the walls, and quills moved steadily in their hands. I followed Eli to the empty desk. On the back of the escritoire was a jug of ale for refreshment. An assortment of quills protruded from the top of the sloping part of the desk. A piece of parchment lay on it, and in front of that was a cup to drink the ale from. There were two seats for this desk. I sat down in the straight-backed chair with a cushion, and Eli took his place in the chair directly in front of the escritoire.

He removed one of the quills from the ink horn, took one of the completed horn books, and wrote on the new piece of parchment. Within a few minutes, he took a penknife lying close by and scraped something off the page. I watched the way he made straight lines and curved others. Before long, the whole page was filled with symbols of ink. He wrote the same words on another page. I studied his writing.

During the recreation of each afternoon, I practiced speaking Latin with Eli.

"Okay," he said. "The first thing we learn will be the Lord's prayer, or the paternoster." He held the horn book in front of me and recited aloud:

"Pater noster, qui es in caelis, sanctificetur nomen tuum. Adveniat regnum tuum. Fiat voluntas tua, sicut in caelo et in terra. Panem nostrum quotidianum da nobis hodie, et dimitte nobis debita nostra sicut et nos dimittimus debitoribus nostris. Et ne nos inducas in tentationem, sed libera nos a malo. Amen."

I practiced reciting the supplication and writing it every day. I loved the prayer. As I said it, I felt good inside. I said it often. I learned more and more Latin prayers and psalms from Eli. He seemed to enjoy teaching, and I enjoyed learning.

Whenever Eli was occupied, I pulled out a piece of parchment I took from the scriptorium and worked on a letter addressed to my uncle. Ambrose had learned Latin from a bishop he escorted on a crusade, and I knew he could read it. I didn't know a lot of words, so I wrote those expressions that I did know. I left space to fill in other words as Eli taught them to me.

"How do you write names?" I asked Eli.

He scribbled down my name, his name, a few other designations, and then Peter's name. I had what I wanted.

Things had changed since my first encounter at the daily meals. Eli showed me the signals if I wanted something. I learned signs using my hands, including placing my thumb and finger together to make a ring. It meant I wanted more bread.

The onset of autumn and winter brought in more orphans and peasants. It also meant less study and more work. Eli taught me how to make candles, tend the gardens along the cloister, and make herbal medicines for the sick. I used crocus seed to treat a man with gout. I no longer saw it as doing petty tasks beneath my ability; I was serving others who needed me. Wasn't that a trait of knighthood?

I awakened on the morning of the New Year. Eli stood over me smiling.

"Today is a day you'll remember," he said.

I thought all the feasts were special. What was different about this one?

The first services of the day went as usual. At daybreak, we entered the nave for Lauds, Prime, and Tierce. When the monks sang, their voices were shrill and out of tune. Eli held his hymn book upside down. I looked at Peter; he made no objection. Most of the monks in the room put on masks. Some of them jumped around during the singing. When the sermon ended, many in the nave brayed like a donkey. I decided to join them.

"Hee-haw! Hee-haw! Hee-haw!"

I looked at Peter, and he didn't move. I brayed until I laughed so hard I held my stomach. Eli laughed with me.

"What is this?" I asked.

"The Feast of Fools," Eli said. "Abbot Peter allows it as long as we don't go too far." Eli brayed again and laughed. "Enjoy it, because tomorrow we must be serious again."

The next day, everything was back to normal. It was as if all the antics of the day before had never happened. Wounded soldiers appeared from the battlefront. I made clothes that day while Eli worked in the infirmary. After Compline, I met my mentor back at the dormitory.

"What news do they have?" I hadn't heard for weeks.

"Monks aren't supposed to tell news outside these walls," Eli said. He looked both ways and got close to me. "Please don't repeat this matter. None of the counties were able to muster together and fight the Tartars. They are killed before they can reach the other barons. These Tartars fight like no one has ever seen before."

I rolled into bed and faced the wall. My stomach churned. Whether I reached my uncle or not, I had to get to the battlefield and fight. I had taken so much time learning from Eli that I had forgotten to practice my yard skills like I promised myself when I first arrived. Starting tomorrow, I had to start my training somehow.

Chapter Six

"Bulls eye!" I whispered.

My arrow hit the small target I made from a blank horn book. It wasn't much. I used a long quill for an arrow and a string of cloth stretched on a wooden bow. It was all I had. I looked around and made sure no one was there. Eli watched. Over the last few days, I had talked my friend into helping me with my training during our recreational time. We found an alcove partly secluded by large bushes. No one came there to meditate, so it made the perfect spot.

"In archery, you must be accurate with your target." I pulled the string back and squinted. I released the small quill and it fell short. "I remember my father's bow. It shot a full furlough." I rubbed the quills back and forth between my fingers. "The arrows were great. The shafts were made from ash wood and their flights were from the finest peacock feathers." I dropped my head and sighed.

"What are yard skills?" Eli asked.

"These are things a knight practice in order to be good in battle." I pulled out a small stick I had found lying in the garden. "There is swordplay." I swung the stick through the air. "You must learn to tilt, parry, throw, thrust, and wrestle to become a good knight." The stick broke in my hand and I threw it to the ground. "I need real weapons," I said. "Did any of the wounded bring any?"

Eli's face flushed and he lowered his head. "They bear weapons when they enter Dayma, but they are not allowed to bring them in. They are kept for the soldiers until they recover." Eli took a step back. "You weren't going to take them were you?" His voice was weaker.

"You act like I've caught the Black Death or something," I said. "Why are you backing away?"

"After all you've learned. . ."

"No," I said. "That wouldn't be chivalrous. I'll borrow them to train with and put them back before anyone notices."

He didn't respond.

"Our people are out there dying. They need help fighting the Tartars. That's the Christian thing to do."

"Will you teach me about knighthood?" he asked.

"First we need the weapons, and then we can truly practice. We'll start after the next chapter meeting."

Eli shook his head.

"What's wrong?" I asked.

"I'm neglecting my duties. I've talked more in the last few weeks than I have in the five years since I took my vows."

I patted him on the shoulder. "Don't worry. You've helped me more than you know."

The next day at the chapter meeting, Peter stood before the assembly and cleared his throat. "Before we attend to church business, there is something we must take care of. It seems one among us sees fit to pervert the holy ways of God and the church. It isn't enough that the ways of the order have been disrupted by disorderly conduct. Now we have worldly ideas being brought into the monastery."

I swallowed hard. Was he talking about me?

"This is part of the disease." Peter held up the letter I had written. "Not only have I found deceit in the author, but also the makings of a thief."

Eli dropped his head low; his face flushed with embarrassment. I wanted to get up and run, but my legs felt like heavy weights were attached to them.

"Adrian, come forward."

I went to Peter, somehow drawn by a force stronger than I was. His face burned purple with anger.

"As a guest, you've been treated with the utmost respect. You've repaid us with acts of rebellion. You were seen practicing things in the garden that aren't allowed in the holy commune. You've corrupted my most trusted monk with your worldly ways."

How could this fat, crippled monk speak of something he knew nothing about?

"Knighthood is better than the priesthood!" I blurted out.

I heard whispers all over the chapter. Peter's eyes bulged in anger.

"Pax Ecclesiae, Treuga Dei!" he said. "If it were not for the church, the knights would still be a bunch of pagan villains plundering villages and killing innocent people."

I knew what he referred to. The Peace and Truce of God was a pact made with knights and the church which brought about the chivalric code and knightly nobility. "You only needed someone to protect your cowardly hides!" I hissed.

Peter shoved the letter into my chest and lit a candle. I jerked the candle from his chubby hand and put it to the parchment. I dropped it in a nearby barrel and watched it burn. All those hours of writing were gone in minutes.

"You are hereby placed in solitude," Peter said. "You'll have no contact with anybody you insolent whelp!"

The whispering stopped. There was deafening silence.

A monk took me by the arm and escorted me out of the chapter house. I heard Peter calling Eli forward. I prayed the abbot would be lenient toward my mentor. The monk took me to the bell tower. We climbed the flight of stairs, and he led me to the top of the building into a small empty room with no windows. The heavy door creaked shut behind me, and all I had was the light of a dim candle to see by. Every time the wind blew, the aperture moved. Surely it was locked.

I picked the candle up, went to the door, and pushed. The aperture creaked open. As soon as it got dusk, I had to leave. Better to die in honor then live in humiliation. I was Adrian of Granes, not some peasant for that holy pig to push around.

Sometime later, I opened the door. Deep darkness pervaded my room. I wrapped myself up tightly against the icy winds blowing and I eased my way down the tower steps. I heard the creaking bells swaying in the north winds. I made my way into the cloister. The moonlight made the frost on the ground sparkle.

I knew where everything was, so I didn't bump into anything. I felt my way around the cold walls and corners. I took food from the kitchen and made my way to the main door. I heard the bulgy-eyed porter snoring in his room. I unlatched the entry way slowly. It squeaked, but it was a low drumming sound. I closed the door softly behind me and turned toward the forest.

I hadn't seen it since the day I came to Dayma with my uncle. Stars twinkled overhead and the trees looked like silhouettes of giant twisted arms. The frozen creek resembled glass. I ran as hard as I could from the monastery. Snow flurries fluttered by my face. I didn't care if I froze to death, and I had no idea where I was going. Everything looked the same. The ground crunched under my feet. I sat down against a tree and rubbed my arms. A blast of icy wind touched my neck and sent chills down my spine. I broke an icicle off a nearby branch and sucked on it. It made me colder, but it moistened my dry throat.

I heard ringing bells.

I got up and ran from them, but I couldn't tell where they came from. Within minutes, I heard the ringing in every direction I turned. It got louder, and I heard the hoof beats of approaching horses. I held my breath.

Two torches lit simultaneously in front of me. Hundreds of men dressed in animal skins and seated on small horses stood before me. They filled the forest and spoke to one another in a language I didn't understand. One of them dismounted and drew his lance. I should have stayed in the monastery. This was it.

Chapter Seven

The soldier stared at me. He growled something at one of the others close by, walked up to me, and looked me over. His frozen breath whipped around his face every time he exhaled. He took the lance and poked the bag of provisions I had. He combed through it, put it under his arm, and motioned for one of the slaves.

"Greetings religious one," the slave said. "The great ones want you to join them in their conquest. You will serve with your prayers."

I looked down at my robes. Had I been wearing anything else, I might have been killed. I had heard the Tartars were very respectful to other religions. I nodded my head in agreement. I had no other choice. I walked beside the one who took my sack. He ignored me completely. My face was numb, my feet ached, and my legs got tired.

After a while, the man held up his hand and all the horses stopped. He dismounted and the others followed. The slaves pulled out coverings, poles, and ropes. They erected tents all around the camp. Some of the slaves built two fires close to one another.

While the servants worked, two of the Tartars stood by the fire combing through a large sack. I recognized them. They were the ones riding through Sir Johns' manor last spring with bows raised. They pulled out human ears tainted with dried blood and laughed. The muscles in my jaw tightened and my chest burned. Could my parents' ears be in there? Did these pagans cut them to pieces? I wanted to grab the bag and run, but I would probably have had several arrows plunge into my back before I made it out of camp. One of the soldiers pulled me by my elbow toward the fire. The bells he wore jingled. He placed my sack in my hand. I dragged my feet across the ground. Were they going to eat me?

"You must pass through the fires," the slave interpreter said. "They must know if you are pure."

I walked slowly to the two fires crackling beside one another. There was enough room for me to slide through sideways without having the flames lick my robe. I closed my eyes and walked between the campfires. The blaze stank from the cow dung used to light them. All the numbness left my body, and tingling sweat covered me. Beyond the fire a chill racked my body as the cold air hit my sweaty skin. The Tartars smiled and nodded. It seemed I had passed the test.

The slave interpreter brought a cup to me. "Drink this. It will please them."

"What is your name?"

He looked toward the Tartars, and then shook his head.

I took the cup and sipped. It was soured milk. I turned my head and grimaced. As pathetic as the milk in the monastery was, it wasn't this bad. I started to put the cup aside, but the slave interpreter clasped my arm.

"Throwing away unfinished milk is punishable by death." I saw the eyes of several Tartars watching me. They wore tunics made of buckram and their braided hair dangled over their vesture. I wanted to throw the milk away, but I gagged it down.

They bowed on their knees and waved their hands toward the moon. I saw a shooting star flash across the sky. The Tartars looked at one another and chattered rapidly like crazed chickens. One of them motioned for me to come to him.

"They are unlucky," the slave interpreter said. "A falling star is a bad omen. They want you to undo the curse."

I didn't know what they expected. I wasn't a magician. I wasn't even a monk. I stood before them and shouted.

"Pater noster, qui es in caelis, sanctificetur nomen tuum. Adveniat regnum tuum!"

I looked around. All the Tartars were wide eyed and silent. I started to finish the prayer, but they stood on their feet and gathered around me like vultures surveying a dead carcass. They pushed me toward a large tent in the middle of the camp.

"You must bow the knee three times before entering an official's tent," the slave interpreter called out.

I dropped to my knee three times and entered the dwelling. A Tartar laid their groaning and grabbing his throat. An idol god sat over his head. I saw a bottle of myrrh among some nearby belongings in the tent, and I mixed it with some wine and gave it to the man. If he didn't have a sore throat, I would be in trouble. They forced me to lie down beside the bed of this warrior. I didn't sleep much that night. He hacked and coughed while the guards came to check on him regularly.

The next morning, the Tartar awakened with a smile on his face. He spoke to his men while pointing at me and his throat. They pulled me off the floor, tied a little bronze bell around my waist, and put me on a horse next to his. The slaves took the tents down and put the fires out. The leader mounted his horse next to me and shouted to the army. The entire posse moved out.

I looked into the distance for any sign of an opposing cavalry; there was none. The leader called for the slave interpreter, and he galloped up to the other side of him. He spoke to the slave and looked at me.

"They are splitting up into three battalions to attack the county of Tiempo. The tumen wishes for you to remain with him for good fortune."

At first, I thought the slave said *tenebra*, a Latin word for darkness. This hard-faced man looked dark. I considered riding away or pulling the saber from the tumen's side and holding him hostage, but I heard Eli's reasoning voice telling me to consider the cost of each action I took.

After traveling all day, we came to the edge of the woods. Beyond it were walls surrounding villages and a castle in an open field. The army stopped with the wave of the tumen's hand. Large catapults rumbled up to the rear of the army. Some of the force went east through the edge of the forest, others went west.

"What happens now?" I asked the interpreter.

"They will send in decoys to open up their gates, and then they will surprise the people inside," he replied.

"Who are the decoys?"

"They are captured slaves who look like local residents but who have defected to the Mongolian army. They send the slaves in front and set their women on horses to make their numbers look larger than what they really are."

I had an idea. "Ask the tumen if I can be the decoy. Tell him I can get him into the castle easily."

The slave interpreter asked the Tartar leader, and he spoke to him and pointed.

"He has agreed to let you go. He wants you to draw the ruler out of his castle."

With a nod from this leader, I tapped the sides of the colt with my ankles. He took off in a slow trot. These horses weren't half the size of Galant. I emerged from the forest and approached the first wall surrounding Tiempo. I felt the eyes of the Tartars on my back watching my every move. One wrong action could have me shot. A guard stood on the wall above the gate.

"What is your business here?" he called out.

"I come from the Dayma monastery," I said. "I wish to see the lord of the manor. It's very important."

My voice quivered. The guard disappeared behind the wall. I didn't know if the Tartars would spring out of the forest behind me or wait until I was through all the barriers. After a few minutes, the gate raised. I made my way through.

"Close the gate quickly," I whispered to the soldiers who met me.

They didn't question my request. They turned the lever and closed the entrance way behind me. I got off the horse and held out the bell tied around my waist.

"What is this urgent business?" the guards asked.

"I must see the lord of the manor immediately," I said. "This kingdom is in danger of an attack."

Chapter Eight

"So you are from Dayma," the guard said.

"Yes."

"What is your name?"

"I am Adrian."

Smoke rose from the openings in the small huts of the peasants. Some of the children poked their grubby faces through the windows to look at me. It reminded me of Sir Johns' manor. A ragged man with a thick beard approached us and held out his hands as if to receive alms.

"Sirs, will you please speak to Lord Vigilan about giving us more wood for our fires? There isn't enough straw on our rooftops. We are freezing at night."

"Get away from us you filth!" one guard said. He waved his hand at the man. "We have more urgent business."

"Just because he is the reeve he thinks he can get anything he wants," the other soldier said.

There was a time I would've agreed with them, but I saw this man and thought of Eli's lost father. I handed him the sack I had. There was cheese and bread in it. The soldiers grunted, but they didn't say anything.

"Why have you built two walls?" I asked. "Why are they shut during the day?"

The soldiers looked at one another.

"There are many thieves in this area," one of them answered.

We came to the second wall. One of the soldiers called out, and the gate rose. As we passed through, two more soldiers met us. The two from the first gate whispered to these men and went back out.

"Follow us," one of them said.

"Are these walls strong enough to withstand catapults?" I asked.

"I don't know," one of them answered. "We've never been attacked before."

"What kind of defenses do you have?"

The soldiers stopped and looked at me.

"You talk a lot for a monk," one of them said.

We stood at the entrance to the large manor castle. The guards disappeared for a moment and came back out. They extended their hand toward the door, and I nodded in gratitude. I entered the great hall and heard a lot of commotion. A man with long blonde hair, long legs, and long arms juggled balls in the air. He was encased in an iron breastplate. A midget with hair covering his body flipped through the air then tumbled across the floor in front of me. Another man strummed his lute and sang about courtly love. The court officials on either side laughed and pointed. Knights, noblemen, and their ladies looked on. I dreamed of being among them one day, but not like this.

The man sitting on the throne stroked his thin, brazen beard and smiled. "Excellent!" he shouted.

The manor guard approached the lord and whispered in his ear. He straightened himself and clapped his hands. The ugly performers stopped. A man came from the crowd, bowed himself, and summoned all the entertainers to follow him.

"Lord Vigilan will see you now," the guard announced.

"Come before us Adrian of Dayma," the lord called.

All eyes fixed on me. I approached him with my head bowed low. I knelt down before the steps leading up to the throne.

"You have news for me?"

"Yes my lord." I raised my head and looked up at him. "As I speak, there is a large army of invaders divided into three groups to plunder this manor."

He leaned forward. "And who are these invaders?"

"They are the Mongols sire. They've destroyed Granes and other counties. Right now they lie in wait at the edge of the forest. They may attack at any moment."

"How do I know you didn't lead them here?"

Did he accuse me? How could he believe such a thing? Would he accuse a monk of treachery? I had risked my life to come here and warn him. I stood to my feet and shook my head.

"I didn't lead them here. I escaped their hands to warn you."

"Strange that a monk would be so bold," he said as he stroked his beard. "It's also strange that a monk would be so interested in the defenses of my manor."

He motioned to one of the knights, and a man approached me and stripped the bell off of my waist. He handed it to the lord.

"You ride onto my estate peacefully with a breed of horse no one has ever seen before, and you wear this strange thing." He rattled it in his hand. "You ask odd questions of my men and you're as bold as a knight." He tossed the bell at my feet. "What would you think?" He wrinkled his thin, pointy nose and rubbed his beard fiercely.

"What are you going to do with him Lord Vigilan?" someone called from the crowd.

"What do you suggest?" Vigilan asked one of the nearby knights.

"Put him in prison until you discover the whole truth."

Vigilan nodded in agreement. "Yes, yes." He motioned for the two castle guards. "Take him to the prison below."

"Please believe me, my lord!"

He turned his head, and I went peacefully with the two men. They escorted me down a drafty hallway with torches hanging from the walls. They unlocked a giant oak door and opened the aperture. It creaked badly, worse than the door of the bell tower at the Dayma monastery. I followed them down a flight of stairs into the darkness. I heard moaning and cries for mercy. The stairs were cold and the air seemed damp for winter.

At the bottom of the stairs were six open cells in the sides of the walls. Light peeked through small openings near the top of each cell. The guards pulled me toward the last hole. An old hag chained to the wall in one of these cells had rotted teeth and looked like skin and bones. She cursed the guards and spat at them. Another was dark skinned and wore a turban. He looked like one of the Saracen I heard my uncle speak of. He sat with his head down and legs crossed. A dirty man with a thick beard and long black hair banged his head against the wall and cried. He gritted his teeth and pulled on his chains.

As the guards took me to my cell, a rat scurried out of it. They locked my wrists in the dingy stocks. Those iron clamps were heavy on my wrist and ankles. I pulled them tight; they were chained into the wall. I sat down on the thin hay covering the floor. Once the guards made sure I was secure, they turned to walk away.

"Wait!" I said.

One of the guards stopped and looked at me.

"What will happen now?"

The guard wiped his nose. "You will rot with the others you liar!"

"Speak to Lord Vigilan for me. If he doesn't do something, his whole county will be taken. You'll be responsible!"

The guard laughed and walked away. How dare they treat me with such contempt! I kicked at them and grunted, but they had already vanished from view. I heard their feet clacking up the stairway.

The dungeon smelled like vomit and urine. I held my breath as long as I could, then I tried breathing through my mouth. If the Tartars attacked this place, I would probably die in here. I leaned my head against the wall, closed my eyes, and said the Lord's Prayer. It had given me peace inside and saved me from death at the hands of savages; maybe it would get me out of this dungeon too.

Chapter Nine

Plop. Plop. Plop. Plop.

The dripping of water from a crack in the wall flowed constantly. I wasn't sure which was worse. . .the dripping from the wall or the whining from the toothless hag. The dirty man with the gristly beard lay motionless with his eyes rolled back into his head. I wasn't sure how much time had passed. Maybe days. Maybe weeks. The iron stocks bore into my wrists and ankles. If the Tartars attacked, I wouldn't hear it from deep inside the dungeon. The bony woman's moaning muffled out anything else.

"Quiet!" I snapped. It seemed as if the dead man's floating eyes rebuked me.

"Who made you lord of this prison?" the old crone whined. "Why is a holy man in a dungeon?"

"Infidel!" the Saracen shouted.

"I don't have to answer your stupid questions." I kicked at a rat scurrying near my feet. "Before long, we'll all be dead like the man across from me."

"Do not speak to me like that!" the Saracen said. "I will cut out your tongue!"

"See the one across from you?" the woman asked. "He was once a knight. Some say devils tormented him. I think he faked to escape punishment. They caught him riding a strange horse and carrying the crest of Granes."

"Did you say Granes?" My heart flipped. The man's muscular body had limped over and fresh spittle soaked the thick beard beneath his chin. This man didn't even look noble. Uncle Ambrose told me Granes was completely destroyed. This man was probably insane. Besides, the old crone probably didn't know what the crest of Granes was. There was one way to find out. "What did the crest look like?"

"A golden lion with paws raised in strike," she said. "They caught him just before winter."

I felt a lump in my throat. He had probably looted what was left from the carnage of my father's manor. It didn't make sense. The Tartars took all treasures with them, or did they? I had to know more.

"What else do you know?"

"That's all," the woman squealed. "No one knew his name, where he came from, or what he saw. Every time they questioned him, he foamed at the mouth and banged his head against the wall."

"Then tell me what. . ."

"I know nothing else!"

"At least tell me what they did with the crest of Granes."

"It disappeared," she said. "That is all I know."

I gazed at the lifeless body across the dungeon. How I wish I knew the secrets he took with him! Was this man really mad, or had he known something? Orange beams of light moved along the wall until shafts of moonbeams replaced them. The only sounds in the prison were the rustling of rodents through the straw. My eyes grew heavy. I curled up into a ball and nodded off.

The huge door at the top of the stairs creaked and awakened me. I heard footsteps. The hag moaned in her sleep. As the visitor neared my cell, a pleasant odor filled my nostrils. It smelled like sweet fruit and nectar. A veiled figure stood before me wearing a gleaming white dress which flowed to the floor. The robes sparkled in the moonlight. An inset dangled from slender arms and waved in the draft of the dungeon. It looked like wings. A soft, feminine voice spoke behind the veil.

"Are you the one who stood up to Lord Vigilan?"

"I. . .um. . ." I was awestruck by this vision. Would someone so beautiful visit me in such a filthy place? Maybe God heard my prayers. "I tried to warn him of the danger outside." I rubbed my eyes in disbelief. "Did God send you?"

I heard a giggle. "Yes," she said. "I am your angel. I was curious to see a monk who knows the ways of the world. It isn't often monks show such boldness, especially toward a lord."

"I'm not really a monk." I lowered my voice. "I only stayed at the Dayma monastery because my uncle was to return for me. He never came, so I went looking for him."

"There is no need to speak softly," the angel said. She turned her head toward the cells of the old hag and the Saracen. "I have placed them in a deep sleep."

"Then get me out of here."

"Who are you?" the ghostly figure asked.

"I am Adrian, the son of Baron Andrew of Granes. The Mongols killed my parents and destroyed my father's kingdom, but I never saw it. I lived with Sir Johns, one of my father's knights, while training to be a knight. When the Mongols pillaged Sir Johns' manor, I escaped with my Uncle Ambrose." I coughed. "He tried to warn my master about the invasion, but it was too late. Ambrose left me at the Dayma monastery and promised to return for me. When I ran away from the monastery, the Mongols found me in the woods and took me with them. They thought I was a monk, and I decided it was best to act as such. Right now they're planning to take this county and no one believes me."

"Did you say Ambrose, as in Sir Ambrose?"

"Yes," I said. I didn't think angels took notice of knights.

"How do you know they plan to invade?"

"They kept me near the leader and told me their plans. I managed to get away to warn the lord, but he thought I was a spy."

There was silence. Perhaps she wondered why the enemy Tartars trusted me, so I thought I needed to explain. I shook my robe. "This saved me. Since they considered me to be a monk, they took me along for good luck."

"I believe you," she said, "and I'm going to get you out of here."

I held my chains out toward this elegant angel. I expected the bonds to drop from my wrists as they had for Saint Peter when the angel rescued him from King Herod's prison. She floated from my presence without saying another word.

"Wait!" I called. "Are you going to get me out of here?"

"Soon," she said. "I promise."

"At least tell me your name."

"I am your angel," came the soft whisper. "That is all you need to know."

Chapter Ten

The wrangling of keys and the patter of footsteps awakened me. I looked around the cell and rubbed my eyes. Was last night a dream? The dungeon remained unchanged. Moisture formed on the jagged stone walls and trickled down it its steady flow. Mud, slime, and dirty straw caked the floors. Straw moved up and down as rats burrowed beneath it to keep warm. Everything was as it had been. A guard with a thick mustache rounded the corner holding a key in his hand. He unlocked my ankles from the stock and motioned for me to hold out my arms. I stretched my arms toward him. He pushed the key into the hole and turned the lock. Whether I was dreaming last night or not, the promise the mysterious angel made came true. Then it was no dream what the old crone told me about Granes and the nameless, insane knight.

"Lord Vigilan requested that you come before him," the guard said.

As the chains fell, my ankles and wrists throbbed from the sudden release of pressure against them. I held my hands up in front of me. Deep, purple bruises scarred each wrist.

The guard grabbed me by the elbow and pulled me to my feet. I hadn't stood since I was put into prison, and my knees buckled on me. I fell into the guard and he shoved me back against the wall.

"You're no threat," he sneered. "You're like a helpless baby."

I lay there, grimacing and signing the cross. I didn't have any fight in me. The guard's hard glance softened and he extended his calloused hand.

"Take hold."

I squeezed his arm and pulled myself up. He bowed under my arm and wrapped his hairy, mus-cled arm around my waist. I dragged my feet and winced with the stinging and burning of my ankles.

As we ascended the steps, I groaned each time I raised my legs to climb. The guard sighed while he pulled me up. When we reached the top of the stairs, he called out, and the heavy door bolted open. Another guard bowed underneath my other arm and helped me down the corridor.

We came to the main hall and walked down another corridor. Violet colored drapes decorated the wall and gothic windows beamed in sunlight from an icy blue morning sky. By the time we reached the end of the hallway, I was taking small steps on my own.

"We brought the monk as you asked," the hairy guard said.

Lord Vigilan sat in a high back chair plated in bronze. He stroked his thin beard and wrinkled his forehead. He held a golden goblet in his left hand. A red carpet stretched from the doorway to the chair. The room had no windows. Lit candles surrounded the walls.

"Leave us," Vigilan said.

The guards removed my arms from their shoulders, bowed in acknowledgement, and shut the door behind them. Vigilan held up his hand as if taking an oath.

"I want to hear the whole story." He pointed around the room. "There are no windows and no cracks in the walls. There is no one here but us. Anything you say will be heard by no one else." He leaned forward. "I'm listening."

"As I told you before, my name is Adrian. I came from the Dayma monastery, but I'm originally from Granes. My father was Baron Andrew. He sent me to one of his knights, Sir Johns, to be trained. After being there only a month, the manor was taken by the Mongols."

"The savages from the east?"

I nodded. "The monks call them Tartars. They wear long tunics, ride small horses, and shoot arrows with great skill. They fight like no one has ever seen before, and they enslave anyone they don't kill." I clenched my fist. "They killed my mother and father."

Vigilan leaned back in his chair. "How did you get here?"

"My Uncle Ambrose and I escaped capture. We went to the Dayma monastery for refuge. He promised to return, but I never saw him again. After many months, I left Dayma to look for my uncle and join the battle. I didn't find him; I ran into the Mongols instead. They thought I was a monk because I wear this robe, so I let them think that to protect myself."

"How did you get away?"

"I pretended to be a part of their plans. The leader trusted me because I had used herbs in previous days to cure his sore throat."

Vigilan stroked his beard and stared at the wall. His face glowed orange in the dim light of the candles. "What is the plan they devised?"

I used my hands and made gestures. "They split into three groups to take a kingdom from the front and each side." I lowered my voice. "They take counties by treachery. They send captured slaves into the manors to create panic or get the inhabitants to open the gates. Once inside, they invade and create chaos before anyone is prepared."

Vigilan didn't say anything. He stroked his beard and held a blank stare. Did he believe me? Did the angel tell him to release me? Did he know about the nameless knight and the crest of Granes?

"My lord?"

He shook himself as if waking from a daydream.

"If I may ask, what changed your mind about releasing me?"

"I was a bit hasty in putting you in the dungeon," Vigilan said. "I felt you needed a fair chance to defend yourself."

He didn't mention my midnight messenger, so I didn't either. I didn't want him thinking I was mad. I had to know more.

"My lord, while in prison I saw a man who was said to be a knight. I heard he rode a strange horse and carried the crest of Granes." I used my hands to make cat claws. "Have you seen it? It is a lion with paws upraised."

Vigilan reached out and grabbed my arm. "We had the family heirloom of your father. It disappeared from our treasury." He released my arm and leaned back in his chair. "The knight told us nothing."

He turned his goblet up and sipped his wine. "I wasn't sure before, but now I am."

"What is it lord?"

He stood up. "You're supposed to be dead."

My mouth flew open. I wanted to say something, but no sound came out. The hair on my arms stood up and chills ran over me. Maybe I was the ghost. Why did Lord Vigilan think that?

"My lord, why do you. . ."

The door to the private area burst open with the two soldiers who had carried me into this meeting. Light from the outside flooded the room and blinded me. Their eyes widened and they breathed heavy.

"What is it?" Vigilan asked.

The hairy guard spoke between deep breaths. "The Mongols. . .they. . .are . . .attacking!"

Chapter Eleven

The sounds were familiar. Men, women, and children screamed. The smell of smoke permeated the air. Vigilan put a napkin to his face and waved his other arm frantically. Four knights stormed into the room and stood around the lord. One knight wore armor that gleamed like a shiny silver coin in the noonday sun. His sword seemed to cut the air around it. The second knight wore bronze armor and a horned helmet. He gripped his axe with both hands. The third knight wore thick black armor resembling iron. He held a large mallet. The fourth knight resembled a golden statue, and he twirled a jagged wooded spear with both hands.

"What should we do?" Vigilan asked.

"Your foot soldiers are engaging the horsemen," the golden knight said.

"We're here to get you to safety," the bronze knight said.

"Why are we running?" Vigilan asked. "I'm not a coward. Are we handing over the kingdom?"

"Our scouts were ambushed," the bronze knight said. "They surprised us."

"They thought our scouts were soldiers," the golden knight said. "Those dogs used them to get through the main wall."

"What about Wensla?" Vigilan asked. "If anything happens to my only daughter I'll. . ."

"She is being escorted by your court soldiers," the silver knight said. "They'll meet us at the underground entrance."

"Who is this ragged child?" the black knight asked. He raised his hammer over my head.

I put my hands up in defense and turned my head away.

"Wait!" Vigilan ordered. "He is a friend. Bring him along."

"As you wish," the black knight muttered. He pulled me into the cluster and resumed his defensive stance.

The golden knight extended his lance. "Let's move. Those pagans are getting closer."

We walked down the corridor to the main hall. One knight walked in front of us, one walked behind us, the other two stood on each side. Each knight had their weapons ready and turned their heads back and forth constantly. We entered the main hall and heard the rumbling of horses and the screams of peasants. A side entrance on the great hall bolted open.

"Protect the lord!" the golden knight said.

A dirty peasant crawled into the hallway sobbing. Three arrows protruded from his back and streams of blood flowed from each wound. Blood poured from the place on the side of his head where his ear had been. Tears ran down his face and he begged Vigilan for help. Vigilan turned his head away and put the napkin to his face.

"I will end his suffering," the silver knight said. He ran to the mangled body and thrust his sword downward between the shoulder blades. The sword ran red with blood as he pulled it out. The squirming body stopped moving.

"We must hurry!" the golden knight said.

I hobbled as fast as I could on my battered ankles. I didn't want to be slain like the suffering peasant. We climbed the top of the steps leading to the throne and stopped. The golden knight pressed against two large stone blocks in the wall. It moved backward, and a frosty breeze whistled through the dark crack. The golden knight took a nearby torch from the wall and peered into the opening.

"Sire!"

Two guards scurried toward us with a maiden in a scarlet dress between them. It had to be Vigilan's daughter Wensla. Her crystal blue eyes sparkled and her fair, wavy hair bounced with each step. Using the torch in his hand, the golden knight motioned for us to enter the opening. The guards left Wensla's side and charged out of the manor. Wensla made her way up the stairs. Vigilan held his arm out and pulled her into him with a hug. He looked back at the halls, and then nodded to the golden warrior. The golden knight and the silver knight disappeared into the crevasse, followed by Vigilan, Wensla, and the bronze knight. The black knight stood there.

"What are you waiting for?" he asked me. "Do you wish to lose your ears like some fool?"

The main door to the hall pounded with a loud thud. It cracked slightly, and coarse battle cries bellowed beyond it.

"Go!" the black knight yelled. He looked toward the bulging door and shook his hammer.

I slid into the crack against the rough edges of the inner wall. The right sleeve of my robe tore on its edges. The air was stale and the ground squished beneath my feet. I shuffled my steps when I heard rats scamper by. The light behind me faded as the black knight pulled the wall back in place. The only dim light behind me came from the torch he held.

"You move like a slug," the black knight said. "Hurry or we will be captured."

My ankles and wrists throbbed. I had so much to ask Lord Vigilan. Why did he think I was dead? Who was the knight in prison? I had another chance to fight the Tartars, but I was too weak to save myself. Maybe my uncle was right about me being foolish. I missed the monastery. I missed Eli's pleasant manner. I even missed Peter's nagging voice.

"Stop dragging your feet!" the black knight said.

I followed the faint flicker of light ahead of me. The floor sloped downward, leveled off, and then turned into a steady climb. The passage became smaller, so I stooped slightly. It wasn't hard; those many months of praying had strengthened my back.

Sunlight poured in from the opening ahead. Branches and vines dangled over the top and the sides of this hole. Outside the tunnel, a stable boy held the leashes of six horses. I waited while everyone mounted. Vigilan and the four knights looked at one another, and then looked at me.

"He can ride with me," Wensla said. Her ruby red lips curved into a smile.

My face flushed and I lowered my head. This is how Eli must have felt. She was a vision of beauty and nobility. I was a bruised, four-smelling prisoner wearing a ragged robe. Vigilan nodded his consent. I climbed onto Wensla's horse in front of her. She slid her arms around my chest and laid her head on my back. I tried to gently pull myself from her grasp, but she squeezed tighter. She didn't seem to mind my appearance.

"Remember my vows," Vigilan said.

"I know father," Wensla said.

The horses galloped in full stride from the fury of the battle. We rode into the lifeless forest where only patches of ice-layered grass and dark wet leaves covered the ground.

"Where can we turn?" Vigilan asked. He stroked his beard with one hand while holding the reins in the other.

"Sire," the golden knight said, "the nearest kingdom is too far away. If we stop, the invaders will overtake us."

"The Dayma monastery isn't far from here," I said. "We can take refuge there as long as we need." Vigilan looked to his knights for approval.

"Lead the way Adrian of Granes," the lord of Tiempo commanded.

I pushed to the head of the group. I knew what I would face going back to Dayma, but there was no other choice. It was the only place we would be safe. It had been weeks since I left. I looked forward to seeing Eli, but dreaded Peter's wrath.

Chapter Twelve

"Here we are."

Before us stood the massive, familiar stone walls and the numerous stained glass windows of Dayma. It was just inside the thin stone wall surrounding it. Everything looked the same. I felt Wensla's grip lessen on me. She dismounted and looked at the building like a child fascinated with a new toy. I dismounted with Vigilan and the knights, and we approached the giant oak door. The huge aperture creaked open, and the bulgy-eyed monk stuck his head through the opening.

"What do you need from. . ." His eyes widened. "Adrian! Where have you. . ."

"I'll explain later," I said. "I need to see Abbot Peter."

"He is meditating in his quarters." The bulgy-eyed monk looked at the knights and disappeared behind the door.

The massive aperture drummed open. I offered to let the others enter first.

Vigilan shook his head. "We are visitors. This is your home. Lead the way."

I walked ahead of them and entered the cloister. We walked down the pathway toward the abbot's house.

"This place is so beautiful," Wensla said.

I had felt the same awe the first time I laid eyes on the buildings. Her sweet voice made me feel warm all over. I still felt her graceful arms wrapped around me from when we had been riding earlier. She was so beautiful. I wanted more than ever to be a knight and impress this fair lady. We entered the abbot's quarters and found Peter sitting in his chair.

"Is that you Adrian, my son?"

Peter stumbled toward us, limping on his left leg. Eli sat across from him at the table. A roaring fire crackled in the chimney. It was like looking on long lost family. Eli grinned from ear to ear, but Peter frowned. When he saw Vigilan and the knights of Tiempo, he offered them seats around his table.

"Bring food and wine for our guests," Peter told Eli.

"Yes abbot," Eli answered.

"I see you have found the prodigal son my lord," Peter said to Vigilan.

The lord of Tiempo chuckled. "It was he who warned us of the invading Mongols. Although they took my county by surprise, we were saved from total defeat because of his bravery."

Peter studied me with piercing looks. I was certain he would punish me, but he wouldn't do so in front of guests. He turned to Vigilan. "Forgive my manners. I'm Abbot Peter. What do you seek here?"

"I'm Lord Vigilan of Tiempo, these are my knights, and this is my daughter Wensla. We are tired and famished. We seek food and shelter for the night."

"You shall have it," Peter said. His jowls jiggled as he spoke. "Anything more?"

Vigilan stroked his beard and wrinkled his forehead. "Ah yes. There is something else."

"Yes?"

"If there are any soldiers in your guest house or infirmary that are fit for battle, I would like to have them. I'm building an army to regain my kingdom and the others that have fallen." He turned to Wensla. "I understand you have women's quarters in this monastery."

"We do lord," Peter said.

"Wensla must stay here until I return. If I perish, she must remain here until my county is restored to her rulership."

"No father," Wensla protested. "Don't talk like that. You'll get your county back, and I'm going to help."

"You'll do no such thing," Vigilan said. "A battlefield is no place for a young lady. Since your mother died, you're all I have left."

"I'm not a child anymore."

Vigilan and Wensla argued back and forth over her role. I didn't hear what they said; their squabble reminded me of the same conversation I had nearly a year ago with my uncle. The last time I saw Ambrose, he was leaving this monastery. Why didn't he come back? Was he captured or killed? What did Vigilan try to tell me in private?

Vigilan and Wensla continued to argue. Three of the knights shook their heads as they looked on. The black knight sat in the corner polishing his hammer. He never removed his helmet. Eli entered the room carrying a tray with bread and a wine pitcher. He placed a plate and a cup in front of each of us, then distributed the bread and poured the wine.

Everyone ate in silence except for the black knight. He continued to sit in the corner polishing his mallet and humming a warrior's song. He remained in his full suit of armor. Wensla snarled when she looked at her father, but her frown turned into a smile when her eyes met mine. Peter shook his head at me. I knew he didn't approve, but it was none of his business. I wasn't going to be celibate. I wanted Wensla to be mine, and what better way to win her heart than by helping her father regain his kingdom and vanquish the Tartars?

"When will you be taking leave?" I asked.

Vigilan looked at me and brushed crumbs out of his beard. "We will depart as soon as all the available soldiers in the monastery are ready."

"If we are to get an advantage, we must leave no later than tomorrow," the golden knight said.

"Excellent," Vigilan said. He turned to the abbot. "We would like to stay overnight."

"We have restored our guest house," Peter said. "You can stay there. Wensla may stay in the women's guest quarters of the abbey." He cleared his throat and wiped his brow. "The hostillar who was keeping the quarters has taken ill. If you need anything, come to me."

"May Adrian stay with us this evening?" Vigilan asked.

"If you wish," Peter replied.

"I'm no babysitter!" the black knight growled.

That evening Vigilan beckoned for me to join him outside the guest house.

"I wish to join your army and find my uncle," I said. My chance to get revenge had finally come. I had so much to ask.

"I never finished what I was telling you." Vigilan motioned for the silver knight and he joined us. "Your uncle Ambrose wouldn't have come back for you. He led the Mongols into your father's kingdom. He told everyone you were killed with your parents."

I took a step back. Sir Ambrose? He was my father's brother. Vigilan was wrong.

"It's true," the silver knight said. "I was in Granes when your uncle turned your father over to the Mongols. Ambrose wanted Andrew's county. He led them to the other manors in exchange for Granes. The Mongols must have promised him your father's estate for helping them."

"Then the knight in the prison. . ."

". . .was a traitor from Sir Ambrose's army," Vigilan finished.

"Then where did the angel come from?"

Vigilan and the silver knight looked at one another, then at me.

"I was merely jesting," I lied. Maybe that was a dream from God known only to me. I wouldn't mention it again. How could my uncle do such a thing? My father was more than gracious to him. Ambrose crushed everything I believed in. "I wish to join your army," I said.

"Look at yourself." Vigilan pointed to my wounded body. It was wasted and weakened from being in prison for so long. "If you were not in this condition, I would take you in a moment. I ask another favor instead." He put his arm around me and pulled me closer. "My daughter Wensla needs someone to look after her. These nuns may care for her needs, but she must have protection. Keep her safe until I return."

"Yes my lord," I said. Vigilan was right. I was in no condition to fight, but to win the heart of Wensla while I recovered would be the first step toward knighthood.

The next morning, Vigilan, the knights of Tiempo, and all available soldiers mounted horses and rode out of the monastery. I stood with Peter and Eli, watching them ride out of Dayma into certain danger.

Chapter Thirteen

Two nuns stood at the entrance of the monastery door talking with Peter. Eli had told me about the women's quarters, but I had never seen any women until now. No one talked about it, and no one from the men's side visited there. Wensla stood between the two nuns. She glanced at me with a saddened look. I wanted to take her in my arms and ride away. Yet, here I stood—bruised ankles and wrists, adorned in a ragged robe, and without the skills of a great knight. I also had the humiliation of my uncle's treachery to bear among the nobility, and the punishment from the Abbot of Dayma.

Peter nodded to the two nuns and motioned for me to follow him. We went into his quarters and he barred the door behind him. "Sit down Adrian."

I sat on a bench in front of the guest table and lowered my head. Peter slid into his high-backed chair and rubbed his chin.

"Tell me everything that happened to you since you ran away. Leave nothing out."

I cleared my throat. I kept my head down and told Peter about my encounter with the Mongols, the escape to Tiempo, the imprisonment, the conversation between Vigilan and me, the invasion by the Mongols, and our escape to Dayma.

"So your uncle betrayed your father?" Beads of sweat appeared on Peter's forehead, and he patted it with a napkin.

"How could he do this?" I clenched my fist. My chest burned. "My father bestowed great honors on Ambrose." I looked for a rebuke from Peter; there was none. "There is more," I said. The angel. Peter would understand.

"Yes?"

"While in prison, an angel visited me. She asked me questions and told me I would be freed the next day. I was released just as she said. I never saw her again."

"An angel, eh?" Peter placed his elbow on the arm of the chair and put his flabby chin on his bent wrist. "Perhaps your imprisonment was punishment from God. It will suffice for what you did." He waved his other hand at me. "Go to the infirmary. Eli has prepared another robe and a basin to bathe you wounds in."

My mouth flew open. Was this the same man who banished me to isolation a few months ago? Why was he so unsettled? I nodded to his commands and headed to the infirmary.

Eli stood in the empty infirmary holding a robe and a washcloth. He hugged me. I pulled back, surprised at his forwardness.

"Where are the sick?"

"All of them were taken in Vigilan's army." Eli placed the robe in my hands. "I thought I would never see you again."

I took the cloth from Eli. While I bathed my wounds, I told him where I had been.

"Peter has acted strange ever since I returned," I said. "He didn't punish me. He seems like a frightened child."

"Abbot Peter changed," Eli said. "When he found out you were missing, he withdrew from everyone. He partakes in the services without getting involved in anything else."

Did he miss me? I didn't think Peter liked me. This tower of a man now resembled a trembling hermit. How could I have caused this?

"Did Peter punish you?"

"He confined me to my dormitory without food until he could think of a suitable chastisement," Eli said. "Before Peter administered my punishment, he found out you were gone. He had nothing else on his mind after that."

"Did anyone confront Peter?"

"No. It is forbidden to question the abbot. He is doing his service faithfully, but his heart hasn't been in it. We are all discouraged because of it."

"Did you see the girl Wensla?"

Eli blushed and lowered his head. Women were a forbidden subject to him. He wasn't supposed to notice female beauty. "I. . .um. . ." He looked around as if trying to find something.

"You don't have to answer," I said. "I merely wished to know more about her."

He shook his head; his face still flushed.

"She's the headstrong daughter of Vigilan," I said. "Before the lord of Tiempo left, he charged me to keep watch over her."

Eli shook his head. "No one from the men's side can visit the women."

"I gave my word to Vigilan," I said.

"Peter won't allow it. " Eli clasped my arm. "Please don't do anything foolish."

Foolish? Eli was supportive before; why was he turning on me? Maybe he was jealous.

"This isn't foolish," I said. "I'm keeping a vow. Wouldn't God want me to keep the vows I made?"

"Not if it meant committing sin. What you are doing will bring trouble." Eli backed away.

Was this the same soft spoken monk I had left? Peter had become a timid baby; Eli had grown a sharp tongue.

"I don't follow your rules. I intend to win the hand of Wensla."

"You're not even a knight," Eli said. "How can you win the hand of a lady if you're not fighting?"

"Watching over Wensla is the same as fighting to protect her abroad. It is noble. When I recover, I'll go to Vigilan on the battlefield and fight beside him."

"After all you've learned, don't you want to be a monk?"

There was no doubt, Eli was jealous. Maybe he was afraid I would leave the monastery and he would never see me again. I patted him on the shoulder.

"I'm grateful for all that you've taught me, and I'll never forget you."

Eli smiled. "Be careful. Tomorrow Peter wants you working again." He left the room.

I returned to the dormitory quarters and nestled into bed. I thought about the way Peter and Eli acted, what my uncle had turned out to be, my parent's death, the unstoppable Tartars, Vigilan's army riding to engage them, and Wensla. With her by my side, I could conquer anything. I had to get close to her without anyone knowing. I thought of every meeting place and time. I would be watched. Difficult days lay ahead.

Chapter Fourteen

The warmth of spring returned, bringing passing showers, lush green bushes, and plump fruits. The grounds inside the monastery resembled patches of green carpet. Activity outside the buildings meant more trouble in finding ways to meet Wensla. I worked hard while devising plans in my mind. Perhaps Eli and Peter thought I wasn't going to do anything. I did chores, said prayers, attended services, and ate meals without any resistance. Days passed. The watchful eyes of the monastery paid less attention to me.

"Adrian, the granator sent this message to you." One of the monks stood at the door to the workshop holding a note.

Why would the monk in charge of the food supplies send for me in the middle of the afternoon? I took the letter and opened it. It requested that I check the stock for all the incoming injured. I nodded to the messenger and headed for the storehouse.

The granary was a large wooden building at the farthest reaches of the monastery. I passed four monks tilling the soil and mouthing prayers. They never looked up or stopped chanting.

I unlatched the door to the granary. It creaked open and banged into the wall of the building. I peered inside. Several baskets of fruits and breads sat on the shelves. I heard rustling, then a giggle.

"Who's there?"

"And my father trusted you to protect me?" The silhouette of a nun stepped into the light. It was Wensla!

"How did you. . ."

"Shhh." She placed her finger to her lips. "It's my secret. I waited for you to make your move. Since you were so slow, I decided to seek you out."

Her face beamed with beauty. Being in a monastery didn't seem to change her. I was glad of that.

"We have to get out of here," she said. "You're all better now."

I looked at my wrists. While there were dark spots where the bruises had faded, I had not yet acquired any real skills as a knight. I needed time to train. "We can't leave," I said, "at least not now. It wouldn't be safe trying to find your father with the Tartars roaming around." I sounded like Eli.

Wensla pursed her lips. "I should've expected as much. You couldn't even get out of prison without my help."

"What are you talking about?"

"I'm your angel." She flapped her arms. "I sneaked into the prison without my father knowing.

I have my own key to the dungeon in case I want to visit. I wanted to see what a rebellious monk looked like. When I told my father to question you, I knew he would. He trusts me."

"I would've gotten out without your help." Despite my appearance, I was still nobility. She needed to understand that.

"Oh really?" She took a piece of bread from one of the nearby baskets, broke it in half, and tossed me one of the pieces. I caught it with one hand. "Good reflexes." She approached me until we stood nose to nose.

I froze. What was keeping me from kissing her? Eli's warning? The rule of a monastery to which I didn't belong? A knight wouldn't hold back. I removed her head covering and her fair wavy hair fell onto her shoulders. I placed my arms around Wensla and pulled her close to me. She closed her eyes and tilted her head to receive my kiss.

"The door to the granary is open," a voice called from outside.

Wensla pulled from my embrace, grabbed her head covering, and crouched behind one of the shelves. I stuffed the large piece of bread in my mouth and swallowed it whole. It made my eyes water. I grabbed the nearest basket and pretended to look in it.

"Adrian, is that you?" Two monks stood at the doorway.

"Yes," I said. I held the note out while looking in the basket. "This letter from the granator requested that I check on our food supplies." I prayed they didn't enter.

"We thought someone had left the door open," one of them said. "We didn't want any wild beast eating up the stock." They turned and left.

Wensla poked her head around the corner. "I must go before I'm missed. Where shall we meet next?"

I thought of every possible alcove, every empty area, and every shaded grove. "We can meet just beyond the main door of the monastery inside the gate. The porter will be away from his place for a few minutes tomorrow after Nones. I can sneak out then. Will you be able to. . ."

"I'll meet you there." She kissed her hand and placed it on my lips. "Until tomorrow."

She looked both ways at the entrance to the granary and disappeared. I returned to my work, and no one seemed to notice my absence. The next day, we met as planned. She was there waiting for me. I didn't ask her how she got away, and she never told me. It made her more mysterious. Every day we met in isolated alcoves, empty guest houses, and every secluded spot. We never met in the same place twice. We talked about our upbringing and our families. She seemed eager to hear what I had to say. I promised to take her away from Dayma and back to her father. One day while leaving an empty prison where I had met Wensla, I bumped into Eli.

"Peter requests that you see him right away," he said.

I followed my mentor to the abbot's quarters. Why did Peter want to see me? Had he found out? Peter hadn't been out of his house.

"He's here abbot." Eli bowed and left the house.

Peter sat in his high-back chair. He examined me as if I were a stranger he'd never known. "I hear you have been neglecting your duties in the monastery. No one knew why until today." His face wasn't red; Peter spoke calmly. "Someone saw you coming out of the empty prison with a nun, although Lady Wensla is hardly such. You are distressing both communities. Such behavior merits expulsion. What should I do with you?"

Was he asking my opinion? He would not separate me from Wensla no matter what punishment he gave. If he expelled me, I could find Vigilan and join his army. I refused to answer.

"Very well," Peter said. "I've tried punishing you, and you refuse correction. I will have the abbess chastise Wensla."

"No!" I blurted out. I didn't care if I got into trouble, but I didn't want anything to happen to Wensla. Vigilan had asked me to protect her, and that meant inside the monastery as well. I kissed Peter's hand and knelt before him with my head lowered. "Forgive me abbot. I'll do any penance you give, and I'll stop sneaking away."

I meant every word. Wensla's safety was the most important thing to me. Somehow I would get out of here and take her away. Peter couldn't keep me here forever. It was only a matter of time.

Chapter Fifteen

Wensla. I couldn't get her out of my mind. While weaving baskets, I thought of her soft wavy hair. Eating bread reminded me of our first meeting at the granary. Everything I did made me think of her. Peter gave me permission to meet Wensla every two weeks and record all the needed supplies of the abbey for the bursar. I fulfilled my vow to Vigilan in this way without causing disturbances. The only rule I had to obey was not to court the lady of Tiempo.

I pictured myself in full armor, riding off into a far away land with Wensla by my side. The Tartars would come after her and I would cut them down. The masses would cheer as I held the shield of Granes high for all to see. Vigilan's daughter would boast to all her mistresses, and she would reward me with a kiss.

One evening in the dormitory, I caught Eli staring at me.

"What is the matter?" I asked.

"Ever since you've returned to the monastery, you act differently."

I hadn't changed. Peter and Eli were the ones who had changed. "What do you mean?"

"Your heart isn't in your work like it was before you ran away."

I would see Wensla again tomorrow. What was she doing at this moment? Was she thinking about me? Should I tell Eli? He would act indifferently, but I had to tell someone. "I keep thinking about Vigilan's daughter," I said. "I intend to declare my love for her."

Eli turned away and said nothing. Minutes passed. I waited for a response, but he never gave one. It was worse than if he had spoken. I couldn't bear it.

"Why don't you answer?"

Eli shook his head. "You are moving into folly, and you won't heed anyone." He folded a robe and placed it at the head of his bed. "There's nothing to say."

I knew what I was doing. He didn't know anything. He was a poor monk who would never have any of the pleasures of life. If he wanted this kind of path, that was his choice. Neither he nor Peter could force it on me. "Are you going to tell Peter?"

Eli shook his head and lowered it. "I can't stop you Adrian, but I beg you to reconsider. Things don't always happen the way we hope they will."

What was he talking about? Wensla wanted to be with me. God desired that men be joyful, and Wensla brought me joy. Was it not God's will that she and I be together?

The next morning passed quickly. I grabbed the parchment and a quill to take notes. We were meeting in the usual place outside the monastery just inside the gates of Dayma. This was a public spot where we could both be watched. I didn't mind. It was a warm spring day. Birds sang and a gentle breeze whistled through the trees. I picked a red flower blooming next to the monastery walls. Wensla awaited me. Nothing could go wrong.

"How is my favorite monk?"

I answered with a smile. She named the needed supplies, and I wrote with a trembling hand. My heart pounded against my chest. I rehearsed this moment many times in my mind. When Wensla finished, she turned toward the convent. If I didn't move, I would never attempt this again.

"Wait!"

Wensla turned to me, startled by my response, "Yes Adrian?"

I placed the flower in her hand.

"It is lovely." She put it to her slender nose and sniffed.

"Wensla." I knelt on one knee. This was it. I would declare my love for her and she would declare hers for me. We would run away from the monastery and find her father. "I feel deep love for you. I wish for you to be my wife."

Wensla frowned and looked around as if trying to find help. "I must go. The abbess will worry." She dropped the flower and ran into the convent.

My stomach churned. I rose from where I knelt and stood there. My legs felt heavy. I prayed this was only a dream. Perhaps she didn't hear me. I knew she loved me. Had life in the convent changed her? I wouldn't accept that. It would be two weeks before I saw her again.

The time passed slowly. When I came to the meeting place to get the list of supplies, another nun stood there. I didn't wait for a response.

"Where is Wensla?"

"Didn't someone tell you?" the nun asked. "Wensla requested that she be excused from giving the list of supplies. She said you are released from her father's oath."

I wrote down the supplies the convent needed. I smiled for the nun, but underneath my lips, I grit my teeth. How dare she do this! There was so much to say, and now she made me break my word to her father. She knew what I had said.

I returned to the monastery, stormed into the dormitory, and sat there all day. Eli came in that evening and sat across from me the same way he had when I first arrived in Dayma. We sat in silence for several minutes.

"Did Wensla turn you away?" Eli asked.

I turned from Eli and didn't answer. Did he take me for a fool? I had more honor than to admit he was right.

"Since I knew you wouldn't feel like working today, I did your tasks." He smiled. "No one else knew."

Eli sat there with a sheepish grin. He was a true friend even after the way I had treated him. He was more honorable than I. Maybe he knew something all along.

"Why would Wensla dishonor me as such?" I asked.

"Do you know why Abbot Peter allowed you to meet with Wensla?" Eli asked.

That was easy. "He permitted me to keep my vow to Lord Vigilan."

Eli shook his head. "If that were the only reason, Abbot Peter would not have allowed it. There was more." He lowered his head.

"Yes?" I leaned forward.

"Years ago, Lady Wensla was betrothed to Prince Sajan of the Saracens to secure peace. Lord Vigilan had told Abbot Peter about this, so he decided it was safe to let you meet with her publicly and thus keep your vow to the lord of Tiempo." Eli stood up. "Prince Sajan brought an army up from the south to aid the lord in battle. The victory was to be celebrated by their marriage."

Eli left me alone in the room. I pulled my hood over my head and tears streamed down my face. Why would God let this happen to me? I lost my parents to the Tartars, my uncle betrayed me, and now the woman I dearly loved would never be mine. All hope was gone. Perhaps I had been deceiving myself. I was too old to become a knight. Only one thing was certain. My fate lay solely in God's hands.

Chapter Sixteen

The prayers were the only thing that hadn't betrayed me. Chivalry was destroyed by my uncle, love was crushed by Wensla, and honor disappeared because I never avenged my parents. All I had left was faith. If the world would abandon me, then I would abandon the world. This monastery was all I had now.

"I want to become a novitiate."

Peter raised an eyebrow. "Do you realize what you are saying? You want to join the order?"

I nodded.

"Why?"

I signed the cross. "It is the will of God. He has taken everything else from me. It is a sign."

"We shall see. First, I must consider your request and speak with the others in the monastery."

I nodded and left Peter's quarters. Was this what I truly wanted? There was nothing else. I wanted to put Wensla, my uncle, my father, the Tartars, Prince Sajan, and everything else out of my mind.

That evening in the dormitory, Eli hugged me.

"I heard about your decision to become a monk. Abbot Peter told me." Eli sat on the edge of the bed and clasped his hands together. "Some think you are too unruly to be one of us."

It was true that I had caused a lot of trouble in my frequent outbursts, my neglect of work and study, and my meetings with Wensla. It didn't matter what the others thought. Many of them had been unfaithful too. Eli was different. What he thought mattered. "What do you think?"

"I'm pleased if that is what God wills." Eli placed his hand on my shoulder. "We will be brothers."

"I want to learn all the Latin prayers." I folded my hands as if I were praying. "I want to be able to read all of them too."

"That will come with time," Eli said. "Right now you should pray and work hard while the monastery decides what shall become of you."

I had to prove my conversion to Peter, Wensla, and anyone else who no longer believed in me. They saw me as a weak knight, but I would be a strong monk.

The next morning, I awakened early and read from the Latin hymns. When it was time to assemble for Matins, I went through the dormitory shaking the other monks and asking them to get up. Some of them grunted; others smiled at my show of zeal.

When we assembled for Lauds, I sang as loud as the monks who had the strongest voices. This wasn't merely from my mind, but from my heart. I would sing all the pain out of me. I would pray all the pain out of me. This was my life now. I couldn't be hindered by all these worldly distractions and feelings.

During the chapter meeting, I was first to offer myself for work. Peter wrinkled his brow, and then smiled. I made pottery that day and shaped more vessels than any of the other monks. There were round pots to cook with, small saucers to drink from, and large crafts to hold things. I chanted prayers constantly while working. The pain would disappear, and I would be at peace.

I was early for every service, bowing lower than the others. I would be more humble. The precentor moved me up front to be closer to the speaker who read. The homilies would push all the past out of my mind.

During recreation, the other monks meditated and chanted in alcoves. I joined with them. When the other monks finished, they went to the dormitory for a quick nap. I continued chanting and praying. As long as I prayed, the pain could not come in. Eli stayed with me.

"You've shown a lot of fervor," Eli said.

"I want to prove to everyone that I've changed. I want to be a good servant of God and the church."

"May God be with you."

Eli didn't sound convincing. Perhaps he was jealous of my zeal and he pretended to be glad for me. He had watched me all day, making sour faces when he saw the looks of surprise and pleasure that I got from fellow monks. No matter how he felt, I would be a monk. All the pain would disappear.

"When will Abbot Peter make his decision?" I asked.

Eli pursed his lips. “Very soon. For the first six years, you will study. Since you have learned much already, it may not take as long. After that, the bishop will visit and make you a full-fledged monk. You would no longer be under supervision.” He paused and stared at me. “You will continue to study the rest of your life, and you will be expected to share the work of running the monastery.”

If Eli was trying to scare me into changing my mind, it didn’t work. I knew what was required of the monks. The prayers had been the only thing that had given me peace since my parents’ death. There was nothing he could say that would change my mind. I nodded and smiled.

“Well then.” Eli stood up and left me kneeling there.

The next day at the chapter meeting, Peter gave everyone a task except me. I waited patiently and watched as he took a parchment from a nearby table. He folded the letter and motioned for me to come before him. With head bowed low, I approached Peter. If I moved too quickly, it would mean pride; if I moved too slowly, it would mean slothfulness. My past failures would be absolved in this one moment.

“Adrian, it is time for the decision,” Peter said.

I bowed on one knee.

“You’ve shown great fervor in your devotion to the church and demonstrated to all that you are ready to become a monk of Dayma.”

I knelt motionless before him, waiting for the confirmation.

"Although you have proven worthy, I must deny your request."

Deny? He couldn't deny this request. It was the will of God, and it could not be revoked. My chest burned again. Why would God torture me by preventing the one thing that brought me peace? Why?

"Your service was acceptable, and so was your humility." He sighed. "A certain monk thought you should not be one of us, and he gave good reason." He tapped me with his forefinger. "Please rise."

I stood up, sighed deeply, and closed my eyes.

"You will remain with us until the war has been won by God's soldiers."

I left the chapter house feeling totally alone. The prayers had been taken away from me. There was only one in Dayma who could have destroyed my last thread of hope. I had to confront Eli.

Chapter Seventeen

Eli and I were in the cellar preparing wine to take to the kitchen. My mentor gave no expression. He collected wine pitchers and chanted psalms. I stood there. He could do all the work himself for all I cared. Eli glanced at me, and then turned to the pitchers. I continued to stand still. After a few minutes, Eli turned to me again. "The servers are waiting for us."

"Let them wait." I folded my arms and snarled at Eli.

"I thought you were different."

"I thought you were my friend," I said. "You said it was wonderful that I was called to be a monk, yet you secretly go to Abbot Peter and turn him against me."

Eli sighed, lowered his head, and sat on a nearby stool. "At first, I thought it was wonderful that you wanted to be one of us. After watching you, I saw something that no one else did."

Not only was Eli being a hypocrite, he was being arrogant. Perhaps he thought he had some divine gift to read a man's thoughts. How could he be so foolish? Maybe he understood the loss of my parents, but he couldn't understand the loss of Wensla or my dreams of being a knight. "Oh really?" I kicked a small pebble across the room. "What did you see that no one else saw, O great one?"

Eli's face flushed. "I didn't mean to sound boastful. I only meant that I've been closer to you than anyone else in the monastery. I wanted you to be a monk. Ever since I came to know you, I had hoped that one day you would be my brother."

I didn't know whether to believe Eli or not. He sounded sincere. He acted as if what he said were true. "Why did you speak against me?"

"You are not a monk within. You said prayers, you chanted the psalms, you wrote the Latin, and you sang the songs, but it didn't come from your heart."

What was he babbling about? Did he know me better than I knew myself? "It was God's will that I become a monk. He took everything else away from me, so I have given up on those things I've lost."

"You aren't the same man I once knew." Eli stood up. "The Adrian I knew was a chivalrous adventurer who wouldn't accept defeat."

"Maybe I was rebelling against what God wanted." I wasn't sure I believed that. I put my back against the rough, cool wall and slid down to the floor.

"I saw the pain in your eyes, and I prayed for you. Every time Wensla's name was mentioned, you chanted louder or refused to talk about her." Eli sat next to me. "Before you found out about Wensla's betrothal, you talked about her all the time. Since you found out, you won't mention her name or listen to someone who speaks of her."

What was Eli trying to prove?

"That is enough to crush anyone, but then there is the matter of your uncle betraying your father."

How did he know about that? I never told him.

"Abbot Peter told me and asked that I pray for you."

It seemed as if he knew my thoughts. Did everyone know my past? I didn't want to hear this. "We need to take the wine to the servers before we are punished."

"You're right," Eli said.

I stood up and held my hand out to Eli. He put his pale hand in mine, and I pulled him up. I pointed to the large barrels in the corner holding the wine reserves. "How long do you think that wine will last?" I didn't care. I hoped to distract Eli from our discussion.

"Hmmm." Eli pursed his lips. "I once heard Abbot Peter tell the refectorian that someone gave a large donation of gold which would keep the wine and food plenteous."

"Has anyone gotten drunk before?" I handed Eli one of the pitchers.

He dipped it into the barrel. "Not that I am aware of."

"My mother once told me how a lady is to sip wine." I took a cup and tipped it to my lips. "Then her cup she should gracefully lift up towards her mouth that not a gout, by any chance doth fall about. Her vesture, or for glutton rude, by such unseemly habitude. Might she be deemed."

"Your mother sounded like a noble woman."

"Very noble." I wished I hadn't said that; it made me feel lonely. I had forgotten how great my mother had been. She had walked with such grace; it seemed as if she floated everywhere she went. Her dark braided hair was never out of place. She had been a strong, compassionate woman. Even when my father had rebuked me, my mother would kiss my cheek, pat my head, and assure me that I would one day make my father proud. She believed in me when no one else did. I shook myself as if waking from a dream, and I handed Eli another pitcher.

"Why didn't your father teach you to be a knight himself?"

"My father had never given me a lesson. Whenever I had asked him, he would grunt and sigh. He was busy fighting wars to protect his kingdom, so he trusted Sir Johns to do it. Johns was my father's greatest knight." That was untrue, but I wanted to believe it.

Eli handed me two pitchers, and I wrapped my arms around them.

"How well did you know your uncle?"

"Before the Tartars raided Sir Johns' manor, I had not seen Ambrose for months. The last time I saw him was at a banquet my father held for the relatives." I pictured my father standing there, holding his cup of wine high in a toast to my Uncle Ambrose.

Baron Andrew was loved in Granes. His memory had been ruined by his own brother. My stomach churned. "My father was a great man." I sighed. "He was better than Ambrose ever will be."

"What would your father say about your decision?"

I saw my father standing there lecturing me on chivalry. Andrew was many things, but he was never a coward. He had taught me to face every challenge in life and conquer it with the courage of a knight. I didn't answer Eli.

"Adrian of Granes, you are my friend. This isn't about God calling you to this life. It is about running from things you cannot change."

I turned from Eli and headed for the stair way. I pretended not to hear him.

"Make peace with your past," Eli called from behind me. "Then if you still feel the calling, you will be a monk from within."

We walked up the stairs toward the entrance of the cellar. I kept my back to Eli. I didn't want him to see the pain in my eyes. Maybe he was right. Perhaps I was running from myself. I needed to search my soul and get back to the prayers. They would give me an answer.

Chapter Eighteen

During the next few days, I went to the small chapel on the eastern wing of the nave and prayed. Peter excused me from my other duties for the rest of the week. This was the room Peter had put me in more than a year earlier when I had disrupted the service. I had tried to get out of the monastery at the time; my only thought now was to leave my past behind me. The same picture of the saint hung over the small altar. I saw courage in the saint's face. I looked at it many times and prayed for the inner strength this godly man once held.

My belly gurgled. I had fasted with the monks before, but never for a week. It felt as if my stomach twisted around my spine. The only time I left the nave was to sleep in my dormitory. I spoke to no one. Every prayer seemed vain. All I thought about was Wensla or the family I had lost. I didn't want to pray. I wanted vengeance against all those who wronged me. It seemed as if God was deaf to my pleas for inward peace. I wished Eli could have prayed with me.

During my last day of prayer, loud footsteps pattered toward the room I was in. I turned to the doorway. A monk stood there with a somber expression.

"Adrian, there is. . ."

"There is what?"

The messenger monk seemed quite troubled. "There's a wounded knight in the infirmary from Vigilan's army," he answered.

"Who is this knight?" I asked.

"I'm not sure," the monk said. "He is asking to see you."

Why would he want to see me? I had several hours left to pray, but perhaps there was no need. Maybe this was the answer to my petition. I followed the monk to the infirmary. Perhaps the news would be good.

"He's over there."

The monk pointed to the bed farthest from the entrance. I didn't recognize the man. He had dark curly hair and a flat nose stretching across his face. His tanned cheek bore a huge scar on the left side. He stared at the wall as if no one else were in the room. I thought of everyone I had seen in Vigilan's army, but none of them looked like this knight. I knelt beside the bed.

"You wanted to see me?"

The man turned toward me. "I never thought to seek after a weakling such as you." He smiled, and then winced.

It was the black knight! I didn't recognize him without his helmet, but I never forgot the growling voice of the man who lay before me.

"What news do you bear?"

"The Mongols have taken another kingdom." He squeezed his side and winced. "Most of Lord Vigilan's army was killed by those sinners. They took my lord, the knights, and the prince of the foreign army captive. Lord Vigilan sent me to deliver a message to you."

"Yes?"

He gritted his teeth and clutched his side again. "If they are slain, you must take Wensla as your wife and reclaim his kingdom." The knight's gray eyes rolled around in his head.

"What did you say?" I knew what he said. I wanted to hear it again.

"You must wed Lady Wensla and regain the kingdom if my lord is killed." The knight's head slumped over on his shoulder.

The infirmarian took the knight's arms and folded them on his chest. He pulled a blanket over the large body and signed the cross. "We must pray for his soul now," he said. "Perhaps God will remember this man's courage."

My lower lip quivered and I felt numb all over. This must've been a dream. The Tartars would kill them. Any enemy who surrendered to them were treated like slaves, but those who rebelled were killed. Nobility didn't matter to the Tartars.

I returned to the room in the nave with the small altar and knelt once again to intercede. I prayed, but all I thought of was Wensla. I knew she loved me. The only thing that kept her from showing her feelings for me was the oath to Lord Vigilan. I didn't want her father to die, but I prayed for the death of Prince Sajan. After all, were the Saracens not the spawn of the devil?

That evening, I heard footsteps again. I stayed on my knees and looked out of the corner of my eye.

"You must go back to your duties now," Eli said.

I nodded.

"Have you heard?"

"I know about the capture," I said.

"I was speaking of Vigilan's daughter."

I turned to Eli. Despite what he thought, this wasn't what I wanted. Vigilan was a noble man. Perhaps this was the will of God. If so, Eli would have to accept it.

"Lady Wensla is distressed with the news. She knows of the request her father made."

"What did she say?" Eli's next words would prove where my fate lay.

"She didn't say anything," Eli said. "She went to her quarters and locked herself in her room."

My destiny was delayed again. I knew Wensla cared for me. Perhaps she was too smitten with grief to think of the happiness I would bring her. Surely she cared nothing for the safety of Prince Sajan. How could I defeat the Tartars with my limited skills? I needed divine protection. "Will you pray with me?" I asked Eli. I had confidence in my mentor's prayers.

Eli knelt down and placed his arm around me. He chanted the most beautiful Latin prayer I had ever heard uttered by a monk. I didn't pray. I listened to his prayer.

"O Bone Iesu, dimitte nobis debita nostra, salva nos ab ignibus inferiori, perduc in caelum omnes animas, praesertim eas, quae misericordiae tuae maxime indigent." Eli opened his eyes and smiled.

"What was that?"

"It was Oratio Fatima," Eli said. "It is a prayer for mercy."

I knew that prayer, but not in Latin. I needed mercy and guidance more than ever.

Eli stood up and patted my shoulder. He walked to the doorway and stopped. "The prince has a soul too," he said.

It was as if he read my thoughts again. The choices of the coming days would affect the rest of my life, and time was running out.

Chapter Nineteen

"I know a secret," Eli said.

"What is it?" I asked.

"I will show you."

I followed Eli into a small room behind the scriptorium. Days had passed since I had heard the news. There were no new tidings concerning the welfare of Lord Vigilan and his men. I wondered if anyone would ever come. The Tartars might have killed the messengers before they reached the monastery. There was no word from Wensla either. If she were in dismay, I wanted to console her. How could she love a prince she had never seen? The only way I would know this would be from the nun who listed the supplies. Eli tapped my arm and awakened me from my thoughts.

"Here it is." Eli looked both ways and unfolded a map of the monastery. He pointed to a blank spot in the northeastern corner.

"There is small, secluded grove outside the monastery. It is hidden by thick trees. Abbot Peter doesn't know, but I saw him go there many times." Eli got closer. "It would be the perfect place to practice your yard skills."

"How did you know about it?" I asked. Maybe my mentor had a sense of adventure after all.

Eli's face flushed and he lowered his head. "I saw a fawn in the fields and I followed it. The animal disappeared into the secluded grove, and I returned to the monastery when I saw Abbot Peter there." He rolled up the map and tossed it on the shelf.

I looked around the tiny room. A few weathered books sat on shelves lining the walls. They were caked with dust and cobwebs. "Does anyone else know of this hidden grove?"

Eli shook his head. "No one knows of it, except for Abbot Peter and me. The abbot has never mentioned it to anyone.

What did Peter have to hide? I glanced around the room once again. "Perhaps I can retreat to this grove during recreation."

"You'll be the greatest knight ever!" Eli clasped my hands.

During recreation, Eli talked with the bulgy-eyed porter while I slipped out of the monastery. I went through the gate toward the little grove. It was as Eli had said. Thick bushes and heavy branches concealed the patch of ground. Inside the shadowy grove, a moist moss covered the floor. When I stood still, my feet sank into it. Perhaps Peter came here to pray alone as Jesus had done in the lonely garden. I pulled a large mallet out of my robe. The hammer had belonged to the black knight. It gleamed in the beams of sun that poked through the thick leaves.

"Now let's see. . ."

I held the hammer out in front of me with both hands. My shoulders strained as I tried to steady this heavy weapon. The black knight had wielded it with one arm as if it were a small stick. I wasn't even strong enough to hold it. If the black knight had been there, he would've taunted me for struggling with his beloved weapon.

A sparkle shone from a hole near the base of a tree. As the hammer moved through the sunlight, it reflected again. I put the mallet on the ground, stooped down in front of the hole, and put my hand inside. A rough bristled bag poked the palm of my hand. I pulled it out and opened it. Shiny gold coins filled the bag along with a note. I unfolded the letter and read it.

To my gracious father,

It was most kind of you to allow me to stay in your guest house until I could return to rightfully claim my kingdom. Keep my nephew ignorant, yet keep him safe. Enough blood has been shed already. I shall use the enemy to accomplish my purposes, and then I will destroy them. You'll be rewarded with more later. Wish me Godspeed.

Ambrose, the Baron of Granes

I squeezed the letter tightly. The guest house had not been destroyed. The night I stayed with Vigilan and his men, there was no hostillar. Every monastery had a hostillar in charge of the guest house. This must have been why Abbot Peter acted strangely. I wasn't meant to ever leave the monastery again. Were I to leave, I would discover this conspiracy. Did Eli know? Was he keeping it from me? He knew things no one else knew. Would he lead me to a grove containing these evil secrets? Eli knew about my uncle's betrayal. He claimed Peter told him. Did he know of it beforehand?

When the church bells rang, I shoved the bag of gold and the hammer into the hole in the tree and placed the letter inside my robe.

Eli stood at the entrance of the monastery motioning for me. "The kitchen needs water for cooking. We are to bring several buckets."

We went to the large well situated in the cloister garth. It was shaped from giant smooth stones taken from the nearby stream. Large wooden buckets and thick bristled rope lay beside the well. I fastened the handle of one of the buckets to the coiled rope and lowered it into the well.

"Did you find the grove?" Eli asked.

"Yes," I replied. I heard a splash and the rope pulled tight.

"It is suitable for training in secret?" Eli placed both hands on the rope and helped me pull the weighted bucket out of the well. He wiped a trickle of sweat from his brow and bent over.

"Has the guest house ever been destroyed?"

"No," Eli said. "During your absence, it was enlarged to house more soldiers. War brings many strangers looking for refuge."

"Did my Uncle Ambrose leave Dayma after I saw him?"

Eli fastened the rope to another bucket and lowered it into the well. "I don't know. Abbot Peter told us someone important was staying at the guest house for a week, and no one was allowed near there."

I grabbed the rope with Eli and pulled the bucket upward. It scraped the side of the well during its ascent. "What happened to the hostillar the night Lord Vigilan stayed at the guest house?"

"I don't know." Eli unfastened the rope. "Why are you asking these things?"

It was obvious from Eli's puzzled look and the tone of his voice that he knew nothing about this terrible secret. Eli was a trusting soul; I didn't know how to tell him. Perhaps there would be a better time. "I was curious."

Eli shrugged his shoulders. "There are times we have special guests stay in the house. No one is to disturb them unless they request assistance."

I slid an iron pole through the handles of the buckets. Eli hoisted up the front end, and I grabbed the back. We placed the pole across our shoulders and walked toward the kitchen and refectory. The buckets tilted back and forth. Water sloshed around and splashed onto the ground.

Tomorrow I would see the nun about the supplies. I would find out about Wensla's welfare. When she was ready, I would take her away from the monastery and inherit Vigilan's kingdom. Abbot Peter could no longer stop me.

Chapter Twenty

During the afternoon the next day, I met the nun and recorded the list of supplies. The quill and the horn book shook in my trembling hand. How long would Wensla torture me? If she wanted to be with me, now was the time. Lord Vigilan, Prince Sajan, and all their armies were probably slain. The short chubby-cheeked nun wrinkled her brow and named the needed supplies. I wrote so fast and hard that the quill tore into the parchment. After I scribbled the last word, I looked up.

"Please tell me how Wensla is faring."

The nun shook her head. "Lady Wensla didn't speak much when she heard the news three days ago. She has cried every day since. She will not eat or sleep."

"What news?" Had they all been killed?

"Didn't you know? Everyone in Lord Vigilan's army was slaughtered except for the lord himself. All the Saracen army was slain too. Only the prince remains." The nun signed the cross and walked back into the convent with head bowed low.

I returned to the monastery and went to the nave. Eli needed my help in the refectory that afternoon, but I needed to pray. The precentor greeted me with a smile. This tall, aged man had snow white hair, a wrinkled face, and a thin head.

"Brother Adrian, are you assisting us today?"

"No," I said. "I wish to pray in the eastern room."

The precentor nodded and extended his hand toward the small chapel. The tiny room still contained the small altar and the picture of the saint. I knelt, signed the cross, and clasped my hands together. Why did the prince still live? Was God testing me? I thought of Eli's words. The prince has a soul too. I didn't want him to die. Wensla was rightfully mine. Perhaps if the prince was taken captive, Wensla would be released from the oath. I prayed for Wensla and the pain she felt. I prayed for her father's safety. The Tartars had probably beaten Lord Vigilan and Prince Sajan. They probably mocked and ridiculed them. They might have had their ears cut off.

Something inside me burned. I saw my father's face and recalled the agony I had felt when Ambrose had told me about my parents' death. I had felt lonely, knowing I would never see them again, knowing I would never hear the sweet sound of their voices. That frosty night, the two Tartars had combed through the bag of ears they had taken as trophies. I had felt such anger at their disrespect of my noble parents.

Was this what Wensla felt? Had she felt the burning for revenge against the pagans? Had she felt guilty, knowing her father was fighting to his possible death while she sat helplessly waiting at the convent? What if that had been my father? Tears trickled down my cheeks. I wept not for myself, but for Wensla. Her heart was with her captive father, and all I had thought of was my own self. Eli was right. If I truly cared for Wensla, then her happiness was more important. The tears dripped onto the sleeve of my robe.

I knew what I had to do while there was still hope. I left the nave and found Eli chanting psalms and washing plates in the kitchen. "Forgive me for not helping you," I said. "I must see Abbot Peter."

Eli looked up and smiled. He nodded and set the plates aside on the table.

The refectorian, a short monk who talked through his nose, stamped his foot and pointed to the dishes. "You've neglected you duties," he said. "We must be prepared for supper."

"Someone else must do it," I said. "I have a higher calling."

The refectorian followed me out of the refectory toward the abbot's quarters. He kept his head bowed and muttered things under his breath. Other monks gazed at us as if we had committed the unpardonable sin. We went into Peter's house and found him reading.

Peter lowered his book and sighed. "What are you doing?" He slapped the book shut.

"Abbot," the refectorian said, "Adrian was assigned to work in the kitchen today, but he has neglected the work, defying your authority and that of the church."

"Why do you persist in tempting God?" Peter asked.

"I am merely following where God leads me," I said. "I humbly request the refectorian find another to finish the wash." I lowered my head. Even if Peter were a traitor, I respected his place in Dayma.

Peter's eyes widened. "Why should I do this?"

I expected him to refuse. He forced me to reveal his sin. "There is a secret grove outside the monastery with a bag full of gold coins."

Peter turned white. "I grant your request." He waved his hand at the refectorian. "Find someone else to finish his work."

The short monk bowed low and disappeared. Peter stood up and wrung his hands. "What do you want from me?"

"Lord Vigilan and Prince Sajan may yet live," I said. "If they do, I must rescue them. If not, I will return to take Wensla as my bride."

"You. . .you can't leave while we are at war."

I pulled the letter out of my robe. "This letter from Sir Ambrose permits me to go free."

Peter shook and wiped a trickle of sweat from his brow. He nodded.

"I need provisions for the journey." I turned to go out the door.

"Wait!"

"Yes abbot?"

"We were running low on supplies. I needed the money for the good of the monastery. Please forgive me." He placed his hands over his face. "Does anyone else know of this?" Months of guilt had formed bags under Peter's tired eyes.

"God knows. That is enough."

Peter groaned as I left his quarters. Perhaps God would have mercy on his soul.

I went into the kitchen and saluted Eli. The refectorian huffed at me and stepped out of the room.

"What did you say to Abbot Peter?" Eli asked.

"I have permission to leave. I'm going to try to rescue Lord Vigilan." I made gestures with my hands. "I heard they were just beyond the forest near the great lake."

"You will be killed." Eli sighed and lowered his head.

"I will return," I said. "I swear."

"God be with you."

I bowed in respect to my friend's blessing. I collected cheeses and bread in a sack, took a dagger from the storage room in the guest house, and left Dayma. . .perhaps for the last time. . . perhaps to certain death.

Chapter Twenty One

The forest blossomed with budding branches and fragrant flowers. Crickets buzzed, birds chirped, and moose bellowed. I pulled my hood over my head and ventured off with the horse I had taken from the stables at Dayma. It galloped hard through the dense trees. The lake was on the other side of the forest, and I had no time to lose.

The stallion bobbed its head up and down as it moved in big strides. I leaned over and patted the creature for its effort. When I rose up, a limb struck me in the chest and knocked me off the horse. It dashed away while I clutched my side.

My back and chest throbbed. I wasn't sure if I had broken any bones, and I was afraid to move. Without the horse, it would take days to reach the lake. Perhaps I had made a mistake.

I heard the hoof beats of a single horse and the jingling of bells.

I rolled back and forth until I was on my left side. The hoof beats grew louder. I clutched a vine dangling from a tree and pulled myself up. The Tartars were known to kill the weak among them to keep their forces strong. I couldn't let them see me lying on the ground writhing in pain.

An approaching figure bounced on the small colt. The man wore the robe of a monk, and a hood concealed his face. I gripped my thigh where the dagger was strapped underneath my robe, ready to fight to my last breath if I had to. The small horse stopped in front of me. The man lowered his hood.

"Eli!"

He smiled with a sheepish grin. "When I heard what you were doing, I went to the nave to pray for your safety. While I was there, I felt compelled to come to you."

I rubbed my eyes. Was this the same one who followed all the rules? Surely Peter didn't allow Eli to leave. "Did Peter give you permission?"

Eli shook his head. "If I had asked, he would have forbidden it. I sneaked into the stable, took this beast, and came looking for you."

I thought Eli would never leave Dayma. It must have been divine leading. How could he have known of my mishap? Why did such a devout monk risk everything he had accomplished to help someone who had doubted his friendship? I had never known such a loyal fellow.

"What happened?" Eli asked.

"A low-hanging branch knocked me off my saddle and into these plants. The horse ventured off. I injured my chest, but I am okay." I brushed grass off my robe. "How did you know where to find me?"

"I used the map from the scriptorium to guide me."

"You are truly chivalrous." I bowed before him. "I would be honored to ride with you."

"We will look for Lord Vigilan together," Eli said. He untied the bell hanging from the colt's neck and extended his hand to me.

I grabbed Eli's hand and hoisted myself into the saddle behind him.

He pulled the reins tight and clicked his heels into the side of the small horse. "Which way?"

"That way." I pointed toward a narrow path through the forest alongside the stream.

Eli twisted the reins and steered the horse in the direction I indicated.

The cool morning faded away in the afternoon sun. The trickling steam became a steady flow of rapidly moving white water. It slapped against large jagged rocks and cut a path through the forest. In the distance, coarse voices shouted and laughed.

Eli pulled back on the reins, and the horse slowed to a trot. The Tartars stood beyond the covering of the trees. Eli stopped the colt and we dismounted.

I bent back a small branch to get a clear view. Tartars and their tents covered the hillside and the valley where the lake was. Some of the Tartars stood before a cart with a felt idol. They held cups of milk in their hands, and they offered it to the statue. One of them came forward with another bowl containing bloody meat. Eli shook his head and signed the cross.

"Look!" I pulled on Eli's robe and pointed near the idol. "That was my horse!"

A stallion lay near the cart with its eyes rolled up into its head. Its belly was torn open and all the legs were cut off.

Eli clapped his hand to his mouth. “These pagans are vile sinners. May God grant mercy to their souls.”

One walked through the midst of them shouting in their language. The slave interpreter followed him. It was the tumen I had cured many months ago. The leader waved his hand, and three men were dragged before him. The Tartar soldiers forced them to their knees in front of the idol and held them by their shoulders. The prisoners’ backs were turned to us.

“What are they doing?” Eli asked.

“From what I remember when I was with them, they didn’t spare prisoners unless they were craftsmen or clergy.”

Eli signed the cross again. “Could that be Lord Vigilan?”

“I pray not.” I signed the cross too.

The tumen lifted his hands toward the idol and shouted. All the Tartars around the cart prostrated themselves before it. The Tartar leader called for someone in the sea of soldiers and motioned for them.

A big Tartar with two long braids of hair and a thick mustache walked up to the tumen and bowed. He turned toward the idol and bowed. He folded his robe back and unsheathed a heavy axe. One of the prisoners squirmed away from the Tartars who held him. They raised their clubs and struck him. The prisoner slumped.

“We must help them!” I said.

"What can we do against so many?" Eli asked. "All we can do is pray."

I pulled out the small dagger hidden in my cloak and examined it. What was this compared to the axes, arrows, and lances of the Tartars? I threw it on the ground; there had to be another way.

The Tartar soldier with the axe scraped a jagged rock against the blade and turned it to observe his work. He threw the rock aside and stood behind the first prisoner. He raised the axe over his head. Eli chattered prayers as fast as he could. I had to do something. I jumped out of the bushes and waved my arms.

"Stop!"

Chapter Twenty Two

All eyes turned on me. Tartar soldiers sprang up and pulled back bowstrings teeming with arrows. I froze with my arms outstretched.

"Adrian get out of here!"

The prisoner who had been beaten broke free from the grips of the soldiers. Several arrows whizzed by, then the prisoner screamed and fell to the ground. I closed my eyes, expecting sharp points to prick my chest at any moment. The tumen laughed. I opened my eyes and saw him motioning for me to join him. All the Tartars lowered their weapons.

"The tumen wishes for you to join him," the slave interpreter said. "Now he knows we shall be fortunate. You have returned."

Eli stepped out of the bushes. The soldiers raised their bows again.

"Wait!" I said. "He is my friend."

The slave interpreter spoke to the tumen, and he commanded the soldiers. They lowered their bows, and the Tartar leader motioned for Eli.

"The tumen wishes for you to witness the sacrifices we are offering to our god," the slave interpreter said. "They are all nobility."

As I approached, the prisoner with arrows protruding from his body called out to me. A man with green eyes and a red mustache smiled. Uncle Ambrose!

"Adrian!" he cried.

I ran over to him and knelt beside his mangled body. Blood streamed out of his mouth as he gasped for air. I had hated him for what he did to my father, but I did not wish for him to die like a coward. He grabbed my arm.

"I. . .I beg your forgiveness for your parents' death." He gagged. "I didn't want your family to be killed. I only wanted them taken and exiled. These pagans betrayed me after I helped them capture Granes." He looked toward the sky. "God is punishing me. Don't let them take our kingdoms. Don't let them. . ." Ambrose's grip lessened. His arm dropped to the ground, and his head slumped over.

The tumen approached Ambrose's body, pulled out a knife, and sliced his left ear off. Blood oozed from the side of my uncle's head. He never flinched. The Tartar leader held the ear up for all to see.

The muscles in my jaw tightened. I squeezed my fists. Sir Ambrose was a traitor, but he didn't deserve this. I wanted to strike the tumen. That was my uncle he dishonored, and he did it in front of my eyes.

The other two prisoners turned to look at me. It was Lord Vigilan and a Saracen with dark skin, deep brown eyes, and hairy arms. It had to be Prince Sajan.

"Adrian?" Vigilan glanced at me. "Wensla. . .is she. . ."

"She is safe my lord." I breathed deep and held my anger. I pictured Wensla's sweet smile. No matter how I felt about my uncle or this prince, we had to come home safely to her.

"The tumen wishes for you to hear of our good fortune in your absence," the slave interpreter said.

The pagan leader babbled on about the armies they destroyed and the manors they plundered. Eli stood close by with his head bowed in silent prayer. I nodded after every sentence to make them think I was listening.

"Now," the slave interpreter said, "you shall see the sacrifice of the other prisoners."

"Wait!" I cried.

"Yes?"

I hesitated. I could've requested the release of Lord Vigilan and left Prince Sajan in the hands of his torturers. Yet, he had a soul too. Were I in his place, would I not wish for someone to free me? God had kept me safe through many trials. If it meant losing Wensla, I had to repay the same kindness to a prince I didn't even know.

"What is it?" the interpreter asked.

"I humbly ask that the two prisoners be released." I sighed deeply.

The slave interpreter spoke to the Tartar leader, and he looked at me with a raised eyebrow. "The tumen wants to know why you ask this."

I swallowed hard. Asking that question had probably endangered my life. I had to think fast. "These men are cursed. Killing them will bring destruction to your army."

The slave interpreter told the pagan leader and he laughed. He shook his head and grumbled something.

"They passed through the fires already. There was no harm."

"True, but they use dark magic which deceives their enemies," I said. "The only way to break the curse is to set them free."

The interpreter told the Tartar leader, and he raised his hand up to the idol and chanted.

"The tumen is not convinced. There has never been a curse on the Mongols for killing noble prisoners." The interpreter pointed to the statue. "One of our greatest warriors commanded that the enemy should be dealt with in this way." He pointed at me. "Perhaps you are the evil sorcerer."

My heart raced. I was closer to being killed with the two prisoners. The dark leader raised an eyebrow again and looked me over as if trying to determine what I was. The other Tartars looked at me with glazed stares.

"I will prove my words are true." I had no idea what to say. Eli's prayers moved me to action.

"What do you suggest?" the interpreter asked. "You've passed through the fires already."

I looked around. There were clubs, lances, axes, bows, arrows, and the soldiers who wielded them. Any test of that sort would either wound or kill me. I didn't have enough skill to wield any weapon. Birds swooped down over the lake. The vast body of water swayed back and forth. It gave me an idea.

"I ask for a trial by ordeal."

"No!" Eli grabbed my arm. "The church banned those trials years ago. They harmed and killed many people."

"What kind of trial?" the interpreter asked.

I pointed at the lake. "I ask for the trial by water. Throw me into the lake. If I float, then I am lying about these men because the water has rejected me. If I sink to the bottom, then I am speaking the truth, and you must set them free."

The slave interpreter spoke to the tumen, and he nodded. He motioned for a Tartar soldier who approached me with a heavy chain.

Eli grabbed me by the shoulders. "If you don't sink, we'll be killed. If you do sink, we'll be free and you'll drown. Either way, you'll die."

"I can't allow this," Vigilan said.

"That doesn't matter now," I said. "All that matters is that you go free."

The Tartar soldier pushed Eli aside and clamped heavy iron chains around my ankles and wrists. He pulled them tight. It felt like the heavy chains in the dungeon of Tiempo. The soldier led me to the lake. The other Tartars parted and made a path for the soldier and me to go through.

"Pray for me," I said to Eli. I heard the sloshing of the waves against the shoreline below me. Only God could help me now.

Chapter Twenty Three

The blunt end of a saber jabbed me in the back and the Tartar soldier grunted. I inhaled deeply. Bending my knees slightly, I sprang forward and fell into the cold water. It smacked my body. The robe I wore grew heavy as water soaked into it. If I didn't sink quickly, the prisoners would probably be cut up into little pieces. I blew the air out of my lungs and bubbles tingled around the sides of my face. I sank to the bottom of the lake. A school of fish scurried out of my way and I landed on some seaweed covered in mud. The water was murky; all I could see were my chained arms.

My chest tightened. With strained glances, I caught a glimpse of a dark hole in the cliff side. I squirmed toward the opening and dragged my chains along the lake floor. It stirred up the sand.

I entered the hole and my chain got stuck on a long stem of seaweed. My chest grew tighter. I yanked on the chain, but it wouldn't bulge. Perhaps this was my fate. Maybe this was my punishment from God for being rebellious and selfish. I thought of all that had happened in the last year. Instead of becoming an honored knight, I would drown under these waters as a pretentious monk.

The chain slid off the seaweed and I pushed my way through the hole. My head pounded, and I blacked out for a moment. If this tunnel was a dead end, I would perish. My face broke the surface of the water and I gasped for air. There was no light. This must've been a cave nearly submerged underneath the lake. I treaded water while trying to catch my breath. Water dripped from the ceiling of the tiny cave. The chains felt heavier than ever; I wasn't sure I could stay above the water much longer. At least I was hidden from the Tartars. They would think that I drowned, and they would release the prisoners.

My arms and legs weakened from swaying back and forth in the dingy water. I looked toward heaven and prayed for the safety of Wensla, Lord Vigilan, Eli, and even Prince Sajan. Was there forgiveness for the way I had treated everyone?

My toes brushed a small rock beneath me that stuck out of the cliff. It protruded far enough that I could put both feet on it. With strained effort, I paddled over against the wall and stood on this ledge.

If these were my last moments in the world, they would be spent in prayer. Clasping my hands together and closing my eyes, I shouted the prayers as loud as I could in this damp, underworld prison.

"O Bone Iesu, dimitte nobis debita. . ." I couldn't remember the Latin for the Fatima Prayer Eli had prayed, so I recited it in English. "O my Jesus, forgive us our sins, save us from the fires of hell. Lead all souls into heaven, especially those in earnest need of thy mercy." I signed the cross. "In the name of the Father, and of the Son, and of the Holy Spirit. Amen."

After taking a deep breath I began again.

"Glory be to the Father, and to the Son, and to the Holy Spirit. As it was in the beginning, is now and ever shall be, world without end. Amen." I signed the cross again. Surely God would listen to sincere prayers that weren't in Latin.

After praying Fatima Prayer for mercy and Minor Doxology for praise, I felt warm strength from within. I chanted the Apostle's Creed and the Lord's Prayer as loud as I could. Other prayers followed. Tears trickled down my cheeks. God had forgiven me; I knew it deep down. Each passing moment gave me more strength.

After what seemed like several hours, I decided to return to the surface. Surely the prisoners were freed by now. I felt strong enough to venture out of the cave.

"God be with me!" I cried.

I dove into the water and paddled through the dark tunnel. The sides of the passageway felt like soft slime. I swam toward the lighted entrance to the cavern. After clearing the cave, I pushed upward until I broke the surface of the water. The bright sunlight blinded me. With eyes closed, I swam toward the sound of water slapping the shoreline. Within a few minutes, my paddling arms and legs scraped the sandy bottom. I stood up and looked at my arms and hands. They were paled and wrinkled from being in the water so long.

"Aaargh!"

A lone voice pierced the air followed by several voices weeping and wailing. I crouched behind the tall reeds near the edge of the lake and squinted through an opening. The Tartars rocked back in forth on their knees and chattered like crazed chickens. They turned toward Lord Vigilan, Prince Sajan, and Eli. The three of them stood unbound in the middle of the mass of soldiers. The tumen grabbed Eli's ankles and uttered woeful sounds.

"He begs you to remove the curse," the slave interpreter said to my monk friend. The lackey knelt next to his pagan leader and sobbed.

Eli's face flushed and he shook his head. "We didn't put a curse on you. We don't know where the sounds come from." Eli signed the cross.

The interpreter repeated the words to the tumen, and he shouted something in his language and shook his fist.

The large Tartar soldier who had the axe stood up and swung the jagged weapon behind his head. He gritted his teeth and shouted at Vigilan, Sajan, and Eli.

"He said if you don't remove the curse, he will break it by chopping off your heads!" the interpreter said.

"We have no magic!" Vigilan said. He stroked his beard. "How can we make you believe this?"

I took a deep breath and stepped out of the reeds. I moaned, groaned, and rattled my chains as I approached them.

Everyone in the camp turned and looked at me. Eyes widened and faces grew pale. Lord Vigilan, Prince Sajan, and Eli stood with mouths open.

The Tartars ran around in circles. They yelled and slammed into one another as if they were insane. The tumen shouted at them and waved his arms, but no one listened. The Tartars dropped everything and ran into the woods.

"It is the spirit of the healer!" the interpreter said. He stumbled backward over some logs and crawled away on his hands and knees.

The soldier with the braided hair dropped his axe and ran. The tumen backed away and bowed many times before he disappeared into the woods. I dropped my arms and stopped moaning. The Tartars had left all their spoil, all their weapons, all their horses, and everything else.

Eli approached me and squinted. "Adrian, is it really you?"

"Yes my brother." I grabbed Eli and hugged him. "God has preserved me."

Lord Vigilan and Prince Sajan laughed and embraced one another. Vigilan nodded to me and smiled. The prince cut the chains off of me, took my hand, and bowed.

"Let's go home," Lord Vigilan said. "We'll come back for the spoil later."

We took four Tartar horses and set out for the Dayma monastery. Whatever had happened there that day would live on in our minds forever. God had answered my prayers. There was only one thing left unfinished. It was in Dayma.

Chapter Twenty Four

The ride to Dayma was quiet. Only the jingling of the horses' bells and the chants of Eli filled the air. Vigilan insisted I lead the procession. As we approached the monastery gates, the lord of Tiempo cupped his hands to his mouth and shouted.

"Make way for Adrian of Granes! Make way for Adrian of Granes!"

The monastery door swung open. All the monks filed outside and stood before us, and Abbot Peter emerged looking bewildered. He backed away and lowered his head. The convent door creaked open, and several nuns came outside whispering among themselves. Wensla peered around the doorway.

"Father?" She pushed her way through the nuns.

"Wensla!" Vigilan dismounted his horse, scooped her up into his arms, and twirled her around.

Prince Sajan dismounted and bowed before Wensla. She looked at the Saracen prince and nodded.

Vigilan held up his hand and silenced the stirring group. "We have escaped our demise at the hands of the ungodly. God has seen fit to deliver us from the peril of the sword."

The monks and nuns lowered their heads and signed the cross. Eli signed and bowed his head. Abbot Peter continued to look away.

"Our escape would not have happened if not for the chivalry of one of your own." Vigilan extended his hand toward me.

I dismounted and stood before the lord.

"Adrian delivered us from the Mongols. He had no weapon or army; only his brother from the monastery." Vigilan placed his hand on my shoulder. "He was thrown into the lake as an omen to let us go free. During the night, we heard his voice calling from the earth beneath us. The frightened pagans begged us to remove a curse they thought we invoked."

The monks and the nuns stirred again. Vigilan held up his hands to silence them.

"The next morning, Adrian appeared from the lake dragging heavy chains. The Mongols fled in terror, leaving everything behind."

"A miracle!" the bulgy-eyed monk exclaimed.

"Truly," another monk said.

"Where were you all that time?" one monk asked.

"How did you survive?' another asked.

"I was kept by the grace of God," I replied. I bowed my head and signed the cross.

The thundering of several horses shook the ground beneath us. Numerous knights dressed in shining armor stopped where we were gathered. The leader pulled his helmet off and revealed his shaggy dark hair.

"Lord Vigilan?"

"Yes?" Vigilan stroked his beard.

"Greetings my friends," the man said. "I am the Earl of Yakanow. The king heard about the invaders from the messenger you sent. We happen to be in the audience of his majesty, so he deployed us to scout the situation."

Vigilan turned to me, then to the earl. "The enemy has retreated and left behind much spoil. Several counties are in shambles."

The earl rubbed his chin. "We request your assistance Vigilan. We will restore all the kingdoms and vanquish what is left of these enemies."

"You shall have it." Vigilan mounted one of the horses provided by the entourage. "Wensla, I shall return." He looked at me and smiled. "Will you ride with me?"

I bowed before the lord. "As you wish."

Wensla approached me. Her ruby red lips curved into a smile and she kissed my cheek. "You are still my favorite monk," she said. "How can I ever repay you?"

Prince Sajan approached me and bowed. "You spared my life. For this, I hold you in honor." He turned to Lord Vigilan. "There will be peace between us. There is no need for a marriage. I have many wives already." He placed my hand in Wensla's.

Vigilan nodded.

"I will never have another friend like you," Eli said. He embraced me with a hug. "You have truly become a monk within."

"Nor will I find such a friend as you," I said. I looked at Peter. The abbot stood with head bowed. I made my way through the monks and knelt before him. "My abbot."

Peter glanced at me out of the corner of his eye.

I placed his hand in mine and kissed it. "You are forgiven. Let peace be in your soul. God will forgive."

Loud whispers resounded through the group of monks and nuns.

Peter faced me. "I will restore everything." The large monk looked into the distance. "How did you survive the lake?"

I stood to my feet. "As I said before, I was kept by the grace of God."

Peter looked toward Heaven, and then at me. "The Lord be with you my son."

I nodded in acknowledgement. "Thank you, abbot."

"We must be off," the Earl of Yakanow said.

Vigilan motioned for me. "It's time to go Adrian."

I looked to my friends one last time and climbed onto one of the horses. Lord Vigilan and the knights snapped their reins and took off in a fury.

"In the name of the Father, and the Son, and the Holy Spirit. Amen." I signed the cross.

"Amen!" the monks and the nuns said as they too signed the cross.

I snapped the reins of my horse and took off with the cavalry. We searched the countryside and found no traces of the Tartars. Some claimed they had retreated from the land completely. We collected all the spoil the Mongols left. Tiempo was restored to Lord Vigilan and Granes was restored to me. I informed every lord and every earl by letter about the tactics the Tartars used in case of future attacks. When the king heard of my bravery, he appointed me Baron of Granes and knighted me. I buried Uncle Ambrose and the sack of ears in an empty field in Granes. The county servants accepted me as their new leader. Vigilan gave Wensla to me as my wife and Prince Sajan kept his word and made peace.

I never forgot Dayma. Peter resigned as abbot and went north to do penance and find forgiveness. Over time, Eli became the abbot of the monastery. I visited often to pray, encourage the monks, and pay my tithes. The monks always welcomed me as one of their own.

I had made peace with my past. Eli had once said there was a higher purpose in the things that took place. Looking back on all that happened, I believed it too.